# A LITTLE DARLING, DEAD

# A LITTLE DARLING, DEAD

by Jack S. Scott

A
Joan
Kahn
BOOK

St. Martin's Press/A Joan Kahn Book
New York

*Copyeditor: Erika Schmid*
*Designer: Mary McBride*

Library of Congress Cataloging in Publication Data
Scott, Jack S.
  A little darling, dead.
  "A Joan Kahn book."
  I. Title.
PR6069.C589L5   1986      823'.914      85-25151
ISBN 0-312-48845-9

First Edition

10 9 8 7 6 5 4 3 2 1

# A LITTLE DARLING, DEAD

# ·1·

There are stoats and maybe weasels in the woods, and of course they rip the life out of rabbits and small rodents. There are owls and cruel-beaked birds who vie with them for the pleasure of doing it. Violent death is the norm along by this lovely river; but the sentimental tourists and day-trippers prefer not to brood about it. Certainly, they do not give much thought to the possibility of looking down to find one of their own species, bobbing about with blind white face turned upward to the sky.

This is exactly what happened to one of them, a man with bony knees called Rawson. The beard, the balding head, and the other complex physical and mental and even spiritual attributes that made up the entire man were also called Rawson, as was the lady picking her way between the famous riverside rocks when he looked down at the water foaming black and white through the small gorge at his feet and said, early on a lovely September morning, "Doris—come and have a look at this."

"What is it, dear?" she said.

"Well, dear," he said, "it looks like a body."

An hour later, Detective Chief Inspector Pete Parsons stood with his legman Detective Sergeant Wammo Wimbush on the flat rock forming the takeoff point for persons essaying— and a fool or two still does—the Lovers' Leap across the fissure-channeled water and onto the rock beyond, flat like this one but set slightly lower. The doctor responsible for their being here, a fat and fussy man but no fool, was saying: "The contusions, of course, are to be expected, and the abrasions. The bang on the head—not surprising, if she fell in. But the tie—that's a different matter."

"Mm," said Pete Parsons. "Could it have caught on something? Between two rocks, maybe?"

"That's your line of business, not mine." Squat, the tweed-clad, tweed-hatted doctor looked beside the two burly young men, and hopelessly out of condition. "Personally, I doubt it."

"Why's that?"

"Wet material—some sort of barathea—won't run, will it? If you want my provisional opinion—provisional, mind—it was pulled tight dry."

"Strangled her?"

"Wouldn't like to say. Need to get her on the slab, see what the lungs tell us."

Other men were here, close by the body. No Scenes of Crime men as yet, because until and unless this fat man's macabre knife uncovered suspicious matter, there was no crime. The photographer was here, of course, snapping away at all angles, and two policemen with a stretcher, waiting. And another policeman, the one called by the farmer upon whose land Mr. and Mrs. Rawson were camping when they hurried up to tell him of the body. Wet patches on this man's uniform were not dried out as yet. It was he who went down to the black, racing-treacle water, to straddle the body with a boot on two rocks and to put around it the rope with which Mr. Rawson and the farmer hauled it up, he steadying it from below.

"And you can't give us a time of death," said the inspector. A very bright copper, this one. Made detective inspector at thirty, which simply cannot be bad. Chief inspector now, thirty-five and with muscles. Good cricketer, too.

The doctor had already declined to pin definitely the time when the girl plunged into that swirling water. He said now: "Told you, didn't I? Sometime last night, I *think*. Need to get her on the slab."

"Uh-huh." The inspector took a careful step forward, to look down at the body lying on the flat rock. Sergeant Wimbush and the doctor moved with him. "Pretty kid," he said. "Good bone structure. All right to take her away?"

"Yes, yes," the doctor said. For some reason, he sounded testy. Fat men in tweed hats often do. It is probably glandular.

Pete Parsons nodded to the two uniform men standing by with the stretcher. "Tread carefully, lads, mind where you put your feet." A rock surface will not show much; but in a case like this you do not want to find, should accident suddenly become murder, that all the little pockets of loose stone or soil that might have held a heel print or signs of struggle have been scuffed over by the walloping boots of great big policemen. He turned to the odd man out, the local constable who, before he even hauled the girl from the water, put in a call to the station. "Your name is—?"

"Grunlet, sir."

"Uh-huh. You'll go with 'em."

"Right." First policeman on the spot always goes with the body, and must stay with it, or get a solid signature on the official form should he hand it over, until such time as a coroner says he can get shot of it. How else can it be confidently sworn to in court that this is indeed the corpse about which everybody is making such a fuss? This man tramped away, out of bright sunshine and into the dappled light under trees in the wake of the two men with the stretcher, the pretty girl on it covered now with black plastic. The same gauge and quality as council sanitary departments use for dustbin bags.

Very often, when murder is definite or even a mere possibility, the senior officer in attendance also stays with the body, but only until after the postmortem examination. This is because the man with the knife may dismiss and possibly destroy things that are significant to the detective. But there is no rule to command it, and Pete Parsons was not one who went. It disturbed him, the cold and casual carving into bloody horror of the human body. He loved a body other than his own. It belonged to his plumpish, warm and breathing wife, and love for one body leads to respect for the entire marvel of living tissue, and the miracle of procreation, and even death. A policeman sees enough of cruel body destruction in the normal course of his work; unless he must, he rarely seeks it out. So he stayed here while the gruesome little party went off, up the path that would bring it eventually to the road where the police ambulance stood, together with the doctor's car and his own. When they were gone, he said to his sergeant,

"Better have a word with these people who found her, I suppose. Hang on here, Wammo. Don't let anyone bugger about the area."

It made good sense. A bit extravagant, perhaps, in terms of pay and time, to have a CID sergeant doing what any Charlie Constable could do; but there was nobody else here, and in terms of personal prestige it can be more expensive to have abandoned entirely the area from which a body has just been removed, if the body turns out to have been foully played. It was still relatively early—eight forty-five, by the inspector's digital—but the tourists and holidaymakers would be clambering along over these rocks as soon as they had engulfed breakfast.

"Yeah, right," said Wammo Wimbush. If you think the name is odd, you never stood in front of his right hook. Big man, he was. He added, "She'd have been done yesterday, between four and five. Bet you on it."

"Why?" the inspector asked. Not because he hadn't thought of it for himself, but it never pays to ignore the other man's thinking. He may just come up with the subtle variation, he may hit upon a salient factor.

"School uniform. She was on her way home. They change, don't they, at that age? Into whatever they wear off duty."

Pete grinned. This was one of the qualities that helped in his rising, this ability to sustain easy relationships with subordinates, his way of treating them as respected professionals, equal in the sight of God to himself. Not every senior rank can do it. But every senior rank approves those who can. "What do you know about what they do at that age?" he said. "Not running a couple of 'em, are you?"

His sergeant grinned back. "Had a couple of sisters, didn't I?" Arguable, this use of the past tense. He still had those sisters. On the other hand, school days were definitely behind them. "Hated the school uniform, used to change as soon as they came in."

"Clever lad," the inspector said. "More than a set of flabby biceps."

"Bollix," said Sergeant Wimbush. Very cheerfully, you could say this sort of thing to Pete Parsons, if you were his long-term oppo.

# ·2·

He was Assistant Chief Constable, and he ruled over every policeman in the town. The Chief Constable proper ruled the
whole county, with assistants dotted here and there. This one
was a skinny man without much hair, native to this town and
with feet corned and calloused from policing it. Perhaps that is
why he got the job, after a steady rise through the ranks. Although some say that marrying the Chief's awfully plain daughter did him no harm.

He had a paneled office with a very fine desk; in which
and at which he sat, mulling over the postmortem report held
in his hands. Very capable hands; capable of knocking up
shelves at home, or hen coops, or fastening very firmly upon
the collars of pissed-up patrons and hauling them into the Black
Wagon, in the old days. None of which things he had done for
many years. Administrative high rank does not effect arrest,
the shelves seemed solid yet, and he had long earned too much
money to fiddle about keeping chickens. They are not lovable
birds, and both they and their eggs are better bought as
needed, clean and tidy from a supermarket. These days, the
hands were used for gripping golf clubs, for pointing out to
subordinates the way in which they should go, for signing papers and for holding them firmly, as now, while he directed
upon them the full weight of his reading glasses. He said,

"No sign of sexual molestation, apparently. Time of death: condition of skin suggests early yesterday evening—"

Detective Chief Inspector Parsons spoke up, from the depths of a good-looking easy chair. "We believe somewhere between four and five o'clock, sir." He used the "we" carefully, to include Detective Sergeant Wimbush, comfortably seated in a matching chair. All the chairs in this office were comfortable, it is a perquisite of high rank. Down in the CID room the buttocks met wooden slats that left red marks if you squatted too long.

"Uh-huh?" Rising intonation and a lifted eyebrow makes a query out of this very policemanly grunt.

"She was wearing the school uniform. Pretty girl—sixteen—they change into leisure gear as soon as they get home."

"Do they? Take your word for it. How do you know? Haven't got any, do you?"

"Never see pretty schoolgirls around town in the evenings, sir. They're all done up like Christmas trees." Mr. Parsons nodded toward his sergeant. "And he's got sisters."

"Two of 'em," the sergeant confirmed. As if it mattered, for God's sake.

"Uh-huh. Good thinking. On the way home from school. Mm. Did she go home through there?"

"Well—it's not the shortest route. But she could have done—lived on the new estate, other side of the A62." The A62 road touches the fringe of the wood. Beyond it, the country proper begins. Very beautiful country, there was a helluva fuss when they mooted that new estate in it. But they built it anyway. Greed triumphs in the end, and there were backhanders about, the electorate said.

"Walk in the woods, eh? Meeting somebody?"

"Quite likely. Schoolboy, maybe."

"Why?"

"For somebody older, she'd have changed."

"Uh-huh."

Sergeant Wimbush spoke. "We don't know anybody else was involved. She may have tried the leap, missed it. We've had 'em before."

"Not locals," the inspector said. "Young tourists, campers, showing off. We've never had a girl, it's males showing off *to* girls we get. And if she was on her tod, who was she showing off to?" Highly ungrammatical, point jumbled onto point. But it served.

The ACC was eyeing his paper again. The little fat doctor acted always with commendable efficiency. Small and fussy men often do. Barely eleven o'clock, and here was the typed report already. "Fractured skull—could have been caused by blow—blunt instrument—could have struck it on rocks—diatoms—bloodstream—establish death by drowning. Tie—barathea—knotted tightly—marks on neck—either by attempt at strangulation or by being caught—latter least likely, but far from impossible—what the hell does that mean? Hmm." The ACC raised his head, took off his reading glasses, and rubbed an eye with the back of one of those capable hands. "Doesn't commit himself, does he?"

"No, sir," said Pete Parsons. Both junior men had copies of the report and so could follow the Chief's progression; which is why he was able to mumble and skip the details, knowing they were keeping up with him.

"Well," he said now, "I don't feel we can mount a full-scale murder inquiry, not on this. You haven't seen anybody yet, parents or anything?"

"Only the couple who found the body, sir. Campers." With bony knees, both. Nothing gained there, they just happened to be scrambling about. "Name of Rawson, here for a

8

week. And the farmer. I thought we'd leave the parents until after they've identified."

"Yes. Mm." No point, unless you must, in barging bull-headed upon people just back from the mortuary. The ACC knew this as well as anybody. Other of his men would have called upon them, escorted them down—they were probably there now—and would bring them back. Leave them awhile, to come to terms with shock and horror and grief. "Right. I think we'll let you have it for now, I don't want to divert a super if it's going to fizzle. Get what you can—you can use a half a dozen men to help, if you need 'em. Don't squander them, though."

He did not need to wag a finger. His minions knew the form. Only in detective novels written by genteel ladies clad in flowing drapery can a detective inspector embark, apparently with deference to nobody, upon a murder inquiry. A murder team will be led by a Chief Superintendent, his pulse felt every step of the way by his Chief Constable, or Commander, or what have you on top of the totem. But a detective inspector may probe into suspicion of foul play, and can call upon help so long as he watches the cost, in time and money. Forces these days are fully stretched, and policemen these days are paid overtime. And watch committees arise in wrath very rapidly, especially if the chairman just got a parking ticket.

So Detective Chief Inspector Parsons and Detective Sergeant Wammo Wimbush rose up from their comfy easy chairs, and the former said, "Right, sir. I'll keep you in the picture."

"Do that," said the Assistant Chief, and turned to the next item waiting in the in-tray. Paper, paper, all the time paper.

# ·3·

Twenty minutes later, the two detectives arrived back at Lovers' Leap. A solitary uniform man stood guard here, summoned by phone call from the farm when Pete Parsons spoke to the bony-kneed Rawsons, so that he and Sergeant Wimbush could return to the station. This man could not be left here indefinitely, basking in the sunshine without good and sufficient reason; and so far, there was not sufficient reason. The obvious thing for the inspector to do, then, was to return here, for a good root about before the man had to be taken off and the tourist trampling started. He spoke as he came into the rock.

"All right? No problems?"

"Nobody about," the constable said. "Haven't seen a dickey-bird."

What totally false impression slang and slovenly speech can give. There were dickey-birds tweeting all over the woods, they were flying about, they were ruminating, the more thoughtful ones, up in the trees. But the seasoned ear absorbs what it knows it is hearing. "Good," said Pete Parsons. "You can hop it now, then."

Again: Note the entirely absurd picture this conjures. Policemen, of all men, do not hop along woodland paths. They walk away on two legs, even as you and me. More so, if anything.

Skilled men can examine a limited area in very quick time, especially when the greater part of it is rock. In what small pockets of sandy earth existed, tiny plants flourished, untrampled. No sign at all of scuffle or disturbance. Had there been recent rain, they might have found footprints on the soft path leading down through the woods; but even that is doubtful. The path is of leaf mold, which will not retain a good impression. Dry, into the bargain. No help at all. The inspector said, after a short time,

"Nothing to chew on here."

"Not a stiver." And here is another deplorable slang expression. Police forces are riddled with them. It comes from mixing with the criminal class.

"Let's get along to the school, have a word with the mistress or something."


It is a very short distance from the wood to the Queen Victoria School, which caters for girls with nous enough to get through the 11 plus. Here they grow breasts, play hockey, grapple with 0 levels; and, given sufficient passes, press their burgeoning womanliness on, to the glory of A levels and even—oh joy of frabjous joys—to University. In a car you can be there in five minutes, even though you walk up the woodland path to where you parked on the road. The bus takes longer, but policemen no longer travel by bus.

They left the car outside the high wall built around a green hockey field, intended perhaps by the mid-Victorian Education Authority that built the school to keep lecherous males out. Nubile girls, some well worth going to jail for, some lumpy with legs like sturdy British oaks, one four feet tall, rushed about with an alarming clashing of hockey sticks, those not actively engaged eyeing the two men with the interest that leapt alive in sentient humanity at puberty long before there were biology classes. Young men with muscles dot the dreams of every normal girl until she is ninety. From there, she is more and more preoccupied with hanging on for her ton, and the Queen's congratulatory telegram.

Viewed from outside, even in September sunshine, the over-ornate, pretentious building manages a gloomy air. Inside, it is an inconvenient warren of stony passages leading to offset classrooms, but bright. Very bright, in the emulsion-painted style adopted since it finally dawned upon whatever dim collective intelligence controls these matters that some of the anemia, premenstrual hysteria, acne, examination-time collapse, and the odd post-result suicide might be due in part to the sheer gloom engendered by brown paint and a grim head-mistress in pince-nez. The two policemen mounted wide, concrete-balustraded steps and passed into the front hall, fancied by not a few.

Nobody was about. They tapped on a door. Nobody answered. Feet pattered on the steps they had just left, and a lumpy girl came hurrying with handkerchief pressed to her nose. "Excuse me, miss," Pete Parsons said. "Do you know where we can find the headmistress?"

"Godda dose-bleed," the girl said.

"Ah. Yes. The headmistress?"

"Id her study," said the girl. "Tob of stairs. Tagg you. Eggscuse be." And she galloped away, the handkerchief seeping red. The policemen mounted very fine baronial-hall-type stairs. There, sure enough, was a solid door with HEAD-MISTRESS lettered firmly upon it, in gold. They knocked. A deep croak commanded that they enter. They did.

A little woman with suspiciously black hair sat at a large desk. She wore a bright pink suit and her eyebrows lifted at the sight of two dark and potent-looking men. "Gracious," she croaked. "What can one do for you?"

"We are from the police, madam." Inspector Parsons flashed the little wallet containing his ID card. "Detective Chief Inspector Parsons. This is Detective Sergeant Wimbush."

"Police?" the lady said. "Bless my soul. What have they been up to?"

No wonder the fine warp and weft of the Queen's English is unraveling about our ears. She, a senior educationalist, of all people should have said, "To what have they been up?" Of course, she was taken out of stride.

"Nothing to be alarmed about, madam," the inspector said. "Just a routine inquiry. One of your girls, I'm afraid, has been found dead."

"Dead?" An unexpectedly large hand rose to the bosom area of the pink suit. "Dead? Surely not."

"I am afraid so."

"But—oh dear. Which one?"

"Her name is Deborah Hollowbone. Lower sixth." There had been no identification problem. The uniform bespoke the school, and little white tags on garments, hand-lettered in ink designed to go through detergent without blurring, told her name and which form she was in.

"Deborah Hollowbone? Deborah *Hollowbone?* But she is one of our—she is—Deborah *Hollowbone?* How did—an accident?"

"We believe so, madam, yes." Don't start a murder scare, not in a girls' school. Not now, not prematurely. There'll be rockets about if you do, especially if it turns out not to be murder. Letters to the paper, questions thundered in council. That's no way up the ladder. That's straight down the bloody snake. "She was found early this morning. In the water below Lovers' Leap."

"Lovers' *Leap?*" Nobody has to tell any resident of the town where Lovers' Leap is. Schools, in particular, sing still in four-part harmony Dr. Siegfried Figeon's arrangement of the contemporary ballad telling how the original young lovers, chased by her father's men, essayed the leap hand in hand, and missed. Eighteenth century, this was. It's a sad story, lugubriously sung. "Lovers' *Leap?*" croaked the lady, who heard it thrice yearly at concerts. "What was she doing at Lovers' Leap?"

"That's what we are wondering. Did she go home that way?"

"I really do not know. We don't know what they do, once they leave here."

"Perhaps some of her friends could tell us."

"Yes. Yes. What a terrible thing. But not now, they'll be going to lunch soon. I shall have to break it to them; I am afraid you won't get much sense out of them for some time. Would you care to come back? This afternoon, it will give them time to settle. Poor child. Poor child."

It suited Pete Parsons very well. By this afternoon, if he left the return until fairly late, he might know what they were investigating. "About three?" he said. And he need not come in person, perhaps. He could hand over to Wammo.

"If it will give you time. We close at three forty-five." She stood up now. It made little difference to her height, but increased her mobility. She was coming out from behind the desk.

"We won't be bothering you for long," he said, laying one of his winning smiles upon her. Women had been known to gulp audibly when he did that. "We won't need to see the entire form."

14

"I shall make you a list," she announced, and stuck one of those large hands out. He took it and she pumped firmly. She then moved on to Sergeant Wimbush, who had not even played a speaking part, to repeat that act with him. Her own smile was suddenly bright, eager, and as suspiciously white as her hair was black. "I shall see you off," she said. Burned-out vocal chords? Old comedians produce that tone, the ones who could never afford lessons in voice production.

They went down the fine stairs, two heavy cruisers escorted by a pink-painted bumboat. The girls from the hockey field had finished their game and came flocking through the door as they reached it, chattering and laughing together. "Girls, girls!" croaked the bumboat. "Quietly! Quietly!" A sallow-faced young woman built like a wineskin and bringing up the rear repeated the cry. "Girls! Quietly!"

Sudden abatement of the all-gigglers-together chatter owed more to unexpected face-to-face confrontation with two lusty-looking men than to the feminine injunctions. Some of the lasses, if they had ever worn them, had discarded or burned their brassieres and went by with a fine bobble, naughty nipples thrusting at the white school blouses. Their eyes slid sideways, soft lips curved craftily, hips lightly mobile with instinctive coquetry. Others, more demurely confined, and, in the main, lumpier or skinnier, or more rigidly inhibited—the conditions go together—passed with eyes fixed firmly ahead, or cast downward. They vanished into one of the side corridors, the wineskin woman crying: "Pick your sticks up, girls, don't scrape them along the floor. Where are the balls? The balls, the balls! Who's got the balls?" A giggle arose from the ranks.

"We are very proud of our hockey team," said the headmistress. "We intend to beat Hillborough High all ends up, this season."

"Jolly good," the inspector said. Couldn't remember the woman's name. Double-barreled. He knew it well enough. Never mind. "Good morning, madam."

"Good morning, Inspector—er—" she croaked. "Terrible thing. Deborah Hollowbone. Most upset." And she shook hands again, all around.

"Where do we go now?" asked Sergeant Wammo, as they walked in the warm sunshine back along the drive.

"Better see the parents, I suppose."

"Mm. Tell you what—a few hours in here would have you very fruity. Cor! You can feel sorry for these poor bloody schoolmasters who get 'emselves in the dock for how's-yer-father, can't you?"

"You *can*," said Inspector Parsons. "Me, I'm no cradle-basher."

Sergeant Wimbush said it again, grinning. "Bollix."

The obvious route from the school to that new and still raw council estate where the young girl had lived is to do as the bus does: Stay on the main road clipping right across the corner of the town. The go through the woods is to make a very crooked dogleg out of it. You must turn the other way out of the school gates and come down to the town center before branching off, over the canal bridge. And you must do it on foot. No bus goes this way.

No reason why a girl should not choose to walk the dogleg, especially on a warm September evening; but growing girls are usually hungry, they normally, surely, go straight home for a meal. Or at least for a cup of tea, and to rid themselves of uniform. If you are looking into such a girl's untimely death, it is as well to apply to the people who should know what she usually did.

So the car drew up in an area where rubble heaps had been too recently landscaped to have flowered as yet into proper gardens, and the small semi-detached houses stood side by side pretending to be Georgian. The two policemen got out and went through a brand-new gate to knock on a brand-new door. Only the woman who answered could have done with a lick of paint.

She looked crumpled. Not old, but shrunken. Distress dwindles people. Pete Parsons said: "Good morning. Mrs. Hollowbone?"

"Yes. Yes," the lady said.

Again, a flash of identity card. "Police, madam. Detective Chief Inspector Parsons—Detective Sergeant Wimbush."

"Ah," said Mrs. Hollowbone. "You've only just left. I mean—your friends have."

They knew this, they had checked by radio with the station. A car had taken them, this lady and her husband, to the mortuary, and brought them back. The crew, one a WPC because women are very good in this sort of situation, had accepted the offered cup of tea and stayed awhile, ostensibly to drink it but in fact because the police, surprisingly tender in such matters—God knows, they experience enough to have learned how to handle it—prefer, collectively and as individuals, not to leave the desolate feeling with the family that they have been forced into the hideous business of identifying a loved one lying on a cold, deep-frozen rack, and afterward abandoned, just like that. So the inspector said, gently,

"Yes—we're sorry to be intruding again so soon. There are just a few routine questions we have to ask. It's best to get it over with."

"What sort of questions?" Policemen are not so proof as people think against signs of extreme stress: the darkened, shocked eyes, the pasty sheen on the skin, the hand rising to disguise the quivering mouth.

"Nothing of great importance. We can come back later, if you prefer." Perhaps it was a blunder, barging along so soon.

The woman hesitated; stood aside. "No—no—you'd better come in."

Walls, ceiling, doors, light switches, carpets, all shared the newborn brightness; but the furniture had a lived-with look. The effect is not uncommon; people cling to the old furniture when they move house. Except newlyweds and cohabiters, who manage to snuggle up, until the flame dies, upon settees covered in tweedy-looking vinyl and struggle to achieve earthquaking simultaneous orgasms between nylon sheets or on the Orlon rug in front of the flame-effect gas fire. As if life were not difficult enough.

Two people sat in the living room: a lad of around fourteen, on the settee; and a man, forty-five—like the woman, not old, but giving the impression of having prematurely shrunk and grown hollow-cheeked—seated in one of two matching armchairs. Pete Parsons said, "Good morning. I'm sorry to trouble you."

"It's the police," said Mrs. Hollowbone.

"Ah," the man said. The lad, less marked by shock—youthful skin absorbs it better—remained silent, his eyes watching the two big men gravely.

"Just one or two questions. About your daughter. Deborah."

"What sort of questions?" the man asked.

"Routine; we have to ask them."

"Yes. Yes." The man sat forward in his chair and, for some reason, brushed what might have been a speck of dust off the simulated wood surround of the coal-effect electric fire.

"Did Deborah normally come home through the woods? . . ."

"No. Usually she came straight, on the bus. Changed—had a meal—went out. Met friends. School friends. Angie Firth and Helen Jonas, they were her special friends. Well—yes—she did have a boyfriend, in a way. Name of Paul Ross, went to St. Peter's. But nothing serious. Discos, she liked discos."

It was Mrs. Hollowbone who spoke the answers, her man leaving it to her. Well, of course, it is Mother who knows most about her children's habits and associates. Not everything—far from it—but very much more than Father does. A brother may know more yet, but brothers and sisters do not spray secrets across the generation gap.


There are not very many questions you can ask grieving parents, when you cannot state categorically that their child has been murdered. There are policemen thick enough to charge in, great fat feet trampling where angels fear to creep; but they are few, and once the Powers know them as thick, they work in branches where a bullheaded insensitivity is an asset rather than a public-image liability. Pete Parsons was not one of them. These few questions asked, he took his leave. The entry was made, he had moved in with sympathy and without spreading aggro. He could come back, and be accepted in again. Good policemen work like this.

Back in the car, Sergeant Wimbush said, "Where to now?"

"Nowhere to go, is there? Back to the station. Lunch. Might have a word with the doctor, on the way."

But the doctor was unavailable, gone about his business.

Inspector Parsons finally got him on the end of the telephone, just before he left the station again with Wammo Wimbush for the return visit to the school. He said,

"George—this girl. Deborah Hollowbone. Yes. One or two things you might be able to help me with."

"It's all in my report." The doctor sounded snappy even over the phone.

"Yes, I know. But a couple of points are not quite—you know."

"I'm due at the hospital at three. Dammit, I've only just managed to grab a spot of lunch."

"Shan't keep you long," the inspector said, soothingly. "Just a couple of points. This fractured thyroid bone. What's the odds between accident and attack?"

"You've read the report, I take it? Fifty-fifty. Say, sixty-forty in favor of attack. Only because the tie was tightened level—the mark on the neck says so. If it had caught between two rocks or something, I'd have expected it to be up close to the chin."

"Why?"

"Well—she'd probably dangle—struggle to free it. And the current would be tugging—the tie would ride up."

Yes. But this was theory only. Not medical fact, hard and fast. Never mind, let it ride for now, it will all come under review later. "No indication of sexual assault, it says here."

"That's right."

"Was she a virgin?"

"No. Oh, no, no, no. Far from it. Very far from it, in my opinion."

"Thank you, George," said Pete Parsons. "You've been very helpful. Very helpful indeed." Well, well.

# ·4·

He rang his wife before he left for the school. Suzie, she was called, and always had been. She was plumping just a little, but very comely; which is far better than being beautiful. It embraces soft skin and unneurotic eyes, a body warmly fleshed and breathing, at board and in bed, and with legs. Legs are better than the twin broomsticks used for teetering about on by pitiful model girls and the skinny like.

Pity they had no children, they deserved a fair clutch if only for enthusiastic effort; but something was wrong, in one of them or both. It did not seem to bother them, but there is no doubt they would have made splendid parents. And potential for good parenting should not run to waste. There's so little of it about.

He normally rang, at some time during the day. Mostly, he had to tell her not to expect him home until late, because so much of a detective's work takes place in the evening or well into the night. Wise wives and those who love their husbands come to accept it, after a time. The rest, by then, have turned shrew or filed for divorce. She filled a lot of time with other detectives' wives—they'd formed a sort of association—and with baby-sitting for humpence an hour; not for the money, but to avoid becoming housebound. She could have taken a job, and just think of the money they'd have had, because she used to be a very private secretary; but, as she said, and he was glad she said: If she were working all day and he was out all the evening, they'd never meet at all. Well—hardly ever.

Today, he was able to tell her he'd be home early, provided—it is the usual detective's proviso—that nothing cropped up. "School hours," he said. "One call to make afterwards, but it shouldn't take long."

"Oh, goodie gumdrops," she said. "I'll put Madge off and iron the see-through nightie."

"Madge?" he said. "Was Madge coming in?" Madge was yet another policeman's wife. They do need to kill the evenings, and you can't watch telly all the time. If you try, he always rolls home in the middle of the program you have been looking forward to. It will be the climactic last segment of a serial.

"Just for a bite, about eight. Doesn't matter, I'll go up to her place this afternoon, for a cup of tea." These wise and hard-fated women kept their social arrangements very loose. Madge's copper, presumably, would be on a late case.

"Wear the see-through nightie, you're liable to get a bite, all right."

"Promise? Hee-hee-hee. And it's rest day tomorrow—long lie-in."

"What's the name of the headmistress of the Queen Victoria?"

"Queen Victoria *School*," she said, punctilious as befits an ex-pupil. "You make it sound like a pub. Miss Wellborn-Davit, M.A. Cantabs. Why?"

"Saw her this morning. On the way back there now. Couldn't think of her name."

"What's she been up to, then? We always said there was something fishy about her."

"One of the lower sixth-formers. Found dead this morning, in the river. Lovers' Leap."

"Oh no. Oh dear. Anybody I know?"

"Doubt it. Name's Deborah Hollowbone. I'll tell you all about it when I get home. Wammo's just walked in. See you later."

"Bye, love. Look after yourself." And this, in an age of rough men with firearms, from a loving wife to an outdoor detective is more a prayer than a platitude.


As they stepped from the car and walked toward the school's balustraded front entrance, Sergeant Wimbush checked and said, "Well, well, well. Look who's here." Inspector Parsons looked, and grinned as he found a skinny-looking middle-aged man in working shirt-sleeves and a cloth cap coming from the tennis court where a batch of girls leaped about missing forehand and backhand. His trousers bagged but his braces were secure, and he wore battered sneakers on flatly splayed feet. He was about to disappear swiftly behind a convenient bush when the sergeant yelled: "Albert. Oh—Albert."

The man started, very realistically, and came footing this way, lips stretched upward and outward in a beam of pure pleasure. "Hello, Mr. Wimbush," he said. "And Mr. Parsons. What a surprise. What are you doing here?"

"Just keeping an eye on things, Albert. Question is: What are you doing here?"

"I work here, Guv, don't I? I'm caretaker, have bin for nearly a year."

"Well, well, how time passes. Seems only five minutes since I fixed you a lagging." A lagging is three years of porridge. Porridge is durance vile. "Caretaker, eh? That's a turnup for the book."

"Come on now, Mr. Wimbush—I bin out nearly four-

23

teen months." In the smile and the near-wheedling voice was the authentic tone of the old lag. A sort of ingratiating joviality, shaped to the terrible, contemptuous joviality adopted by the policeman who knows him well.

"I thought you were still in. Going straight, then, are you?" The sergeant, too, was beaming. Even Pete Parsons was smiling; but Albert—Albert Fish, his full name—was one of Wammo's old customers, so the inspector stood silently by.

"Yeah. All that's behind me. Got me chance, diden I? Got a good job here—"

"So long as you don't start nicking the netball trophies."

"Lay orf, Guv."

"They'll be missing you in the nick."

"Have to miss me then, won't they? That's all over. I done all me bird, you ought to lay orf the aggro, reely."

"Aggro, Albert? I thought I was being real friendly."

Pete Parsons spoke up. An old lag is one thing. An old lag trying to go straight—he's another. You shouldn't lean on the poor bugger. "Glad to see you, Albert. Glad to see you having a go."

"Thanks, Mr. Parsons," Albert said.

"So's he, really." The grin he spread between Sergeant Wammo and his old client managed to damp down any lingering aggro. "He's a bit slow to move with the times, that's all."

Truth to tell, the sergeant was glad of the intervention. Automatically, coming upon the man unexpectedly, he had addressed him in the style to which both were accustomed; and once committed, he was having to carry it on. Now he spoke as to any other man. "Yeah—glad to see you, Albert. Still use the Rose and Crown?"

"I get in there sometimes. Not a lot."

"See you in there, sometime. I'll buy you a drink."

"Yeah. That'll be nice. I'm in every Saturday. Very nice

seeing you, gents." And the splay feet bore him away; whether on caretakerly duty or to skive in some hidey-hole, who can say?

"Fancy that," said Sergeant Wimbush as the two policemen moved on into the building. "Old Albert Fish. Caretaker. Poacher turned bloody gamekeeper. How'd he get a job like that?"

"Probation Service. After-Care. Do-gooder with influence. Lot of old lags get jobs with the council, it's all part of the policy."

"Yeah. Well—we'll know who to pick up, if the Sponsored Swim money goes missing."

Very unfair. But only the naive nig-nog believes that the book is really squared, once a man has Paid his Debt. Especially if he keeps incurring another one.

The headmistress was in her study, behind the big desk. She rose as they came in, saying: "Ah—Inspector—here we are again, then."

"Here we are again, Miss Wellborn-Davit."

"One trusts you will not need to interview the entire form, the girls are rather apt to—it is best not to overexcite them. I have prepared a list." She picked up from her desk and handed over a sheet of paper; said as he studied it: "Just the three names. Poor little Deborah's especial friends."

Three names only, two of which he already possessed. Hardly worth writing them out. But teachers love a list. "Fine, madam," the policeman said. "Where shall we—?" Until and unless it was murder, no point in a general interview. After all, what was he doing here, really? A little fishing, that's all. Just a little fishing.

"If you will follow me," croaked the lady, who had it all worked out. She made for the door.

They saw the girls in a smallish room labeled MUSIC,

with a piano in it. There were also a flat-topped, well-battered table and several small wooden chairs. Two places were set with note-taking paper and ballpoint pens, and two of these chairs had been positioned behind the table. Three more stood in front of it. If it was not always like this, the headmistress had had it prepared, probably by Albert Fish. She said, "Perhaps you will sit there"; and off she went, to fetch the girls.

They entered quietly, shepherded from the rear. Two pretty girls, one exceptionally so. The other plump and plain, with big, round spectacles, very unbecoming. A common feminine mix, the pretty and the plain. Easy to see why pretty accepts plain: Plain can be used as foil, she will admire, adore. Above all—she presents no competition in the sexual game. Every young actress keeps at least one, and a little snappy dog. Less easy to understand why plain is impelled to seek out the pretty, to flatter and fawn and abase herself into what looks like an humiliating condition of self-denigration. And it happens all the time, with plain prime mover in setting up the relationship. Weird are the ways of God. Or Ms. God, according to your need.

"Here we are, then, Inspector," croaked Miss Wellborn-Davit, on what was meant, obviously, to be a jovial note. "Girls, this is Inspector Parsons. And this is Sergeant Rambush."

"Wimbush, madam," the sergeant said. They looked very big, the two detectives, squatting behind the table on those insufficient chairs. It pulled their trouser legs up, supplying proof, if proof were needed, that the sergeant wore irresponsible socks.

"How do you do," said Pete Parsons.

"How do you do," they said, gravely; very nearly demure in their uniform of white blouse, navy-blue skirt, and blue, badge-embroidered tie. And they all wore bras. Must have done, there was no sign of nipples.

"Sit down, girls," croaked the headmistress, very much in command. "Nothing to be nervous about, the inspector merely wants to ask you a few simple questions." The school had, probably, been told of the death by now. It would account for the ungiggling gravity. In normal times young girls always giggle in the presence of strange and potent men. It comes from interior tickle, and from each knowing what the other is thinking when sidelong glances meet.

"Let's get you sorted out first," said Inspector Parsons. He smiled a smile wide, white, and proved by their later reactions to have stirred up women come to greater sexual stability than they had known at sixteen; directed it at the prettiest of the three. "You are—?"

"Helen Jonas," she said. No blush, no giggle. Quite self-possessed.

The inspector made marks on the paper with one of the ballpoint pens. It is the least one can do, they having been thoughtfully provided. He moved his smile on. No need to ask the question. "Angela Firth," said the second pretty girl, equally composed.

Again the smile traveled. "And you will be Patricia Dixon."

The plain, plump girl murmured, the only one to show visible signs of nervousness. "Speak up, Patricia," cried Miss Wellborn-Davit in the tone of a jolly natterjack toad. "Nobody's going to bite you."

"Yes," the girl said, when she had cleared her throat.

"Good," said Pete Parsons. "I shan't keep you long. I believe you are all good friends of Deborah Hollowbone." He

did not need to say deceased, or the late, or anything empha-
sizing the past tense. They knew.

"Yes," they answered.

"Good. Fine. Did any of you go home with her?"

"Sometimes," they said.

"Yesterday?"

"No," they said.

"Uh-huh. I believe she usually went straight home on
the bus."

"Yes."

"Do you travel with her?"

"No," said the two pretty girls. The plain one answered:
"I do. Usually. I live near her."

"What about yesterday?"

"Not yesterday. She went off on her own."

"You didn't go with her."

"No."

"Did any of you go with her?"

Nobody said she did.

"Did she often go home through the woods?"

A variety of answers: one no, one don't know, and a
sometimes from the plump girl, who took off her unflattering
spectacles to clear them of creeping mist. Emotion might have
caused it, sorrow for her dead friend. Or it may have been
perspiration. The plump tend to sweat, especially when they
are nervous on a warm afternoon. The inspector spoke directly
to her.

"Often?" Often enough to be meeting somebody—a
man? A boy?—regularly? Seldom enough to eliminate that
line?

"No. I don't know."

"Come along now, Patricia," said Miss Wellborn-Davit
encouragingly.

"I mean, she didn't always go on the bus. But I don't know if she went through the woods."

"I see. Yes. What about boyfriends? Did she have a boy-friend?"

Definite hesitation, perhaps because the headmistress was there. Then the very pretty Helen said, "Paul Ross. He goes to St. Peter's."

"Uh-huh." The name was already in Sergeant Wimbush's little black book. With the lad's home address, supplied by the girl's parents. Next and last on the list to be visited. "Anybody else?"

No, they said. Not so far as they knew. He was the one she went to discos with, the only one they knew about.

"Was it serious? Engaged, anything like that?"

Miss Wellborn-Davit croaked up. "People in the lower sixth do not become engaged, Mr. Parsons."

No? They become pregnant, don't they? In junior school, some of them. They sniff glue, smoke grass or worse, break and enter, mug little old ladies. But engaged? Perhaps not, in grammar schools. "No. Of course not." The inspector adjusted his pleasant expression, widening it into the smile again. "Well—I think that will be all. Thank you for your cooperation."

"Thank you," they murmured. Very polite, they were. Again, perhaps because Authority was so present, together with the kind of pungent masculinity that plays upon instinct and countless generations of social conditioning to bash Women's Lib back into nullity in the hearts and minds of young girls. They did not even get up from their chairs, each looking at the others as if for guidance, young buttocks hardly rising until Miss Wellborn-Davit husked,

"All right, girls. Back to your work. Quietly, now; no chattering along the corridors."

"Yes, Miss Wellborn-Davit," they said, and left; two on legs slender as the legs of carefully nurtured fillies, imparting delicate filly-sway to the miraculous nubility above; the other on limbs that might have been grafted from a Victorian dining table, and with no sway at all.

"Nice girls," the inspector said, when they were gone.

"Most of our girls are," Miss Wellborn-Davit assured him earnestly. "I *could* say *all* our girls are. Poor little Deborah. Terrible."

"Was she a bright pupil?" Not that it made a lot of difference. But some sort of conversation must bridge the time between when you rise from a table to fold and pocket a sheet of unnecessary paper and when you leave.

"Very. English subjects particularly. Good all-rounder. Sports. We shall miss her badly in the hockey team. Keen as mustard. Can one offer you a cup of tea?"

"That's very nice of you. Cup of tea, Sergeant?"

"Go down a treat, a cup of tea would," said Sergeant Wammo, in with a speaking part at last. His were the notes that would count, though, if any did; not the scattered bits of ballpoint work on the inspector's scrap of paper. Policemen appreciate the helpful gesture, and will respond to it; but when it comes to notes, they stick to the little black book.

Tea came in Miss Wellborn-Davit's study. She pressed the switch of an intercom machine and said: "Miss Bloomer, will you send up tea for three? Thank you." A few minutes later it arrived, borne on trays with biscuits, thin slices of bread and butter, jams in silvery pots, lemon-curd tarts, and little fancy cakes, by three girls quite similar in basic structure to the three friends just interviewed. "Cookery class," said Miss Wellborn-Davit. "Domestic Science, does us no harm to get a little practical. Thank you, girls. Carefully, now, with the milk jug. Indian or China, Mr. Parsons?"

There was no particular hurry. The station knew where they were, and they had no reason solid enough to justify their disrupting work at St. Peter's by calling unexpectedly upon another head teacher and asking that a boy be tugged out from his form room. So they tucked into the goodies. Homemade goodies supplement very nicely the nutrient intake required by big-boned men, especially such as are produced in gleaming school kitchen-classrooms under the eye of a dedicated gourmet mistress.

By the time they were wiping away crumbs and had drained the teapots, the three hundred and forty girls corralled in various classrooms were packing away their books for the day. Through the little barred window in the basement boiler room that looked out over drive and playing fields, Albert Fish saw the old enemy emerge, chat for a moment with Miss Wellborn-Davit, and shake hands with her before driving away. He always vanished into the boiler room when he needed a cigarette, but this visit was dual-purposed. He needed a quick drag, true; but he also wanted to keep obbo, to see when and in what order they left. Watching, well out of sight, he puffed nervously. It bothered him, having the bastards suddenly appear like that. Old lags are invariably nervous men and it does nothing to soothe them, looking at policemen through a little barred window.

Soon after, the go-home bell rang. Girls in a wild variety of shapes and sizes began to issue from that imposing front doorway, to drift in groups or rush singly along the drive. The three friends of Deborah Hollowbone met at the bottom of the steps, able to gather for the first time since the questioning and to talk without constraint. They waited until they were at a distance from other girls before anybody spoke. Then the lovely Helen said,

"They won't know anything. How can they?"

"She might have kept a diary, or something," said Angela.

"She wouldn't. Would she?"

They walked on for a space, thinking about it. People do keep diaries. Plump Patricia said, blinking through the owl-eye spectacles,

"The jewelry. That's what they'll wonder about. What did she do with the jewelry?"

A further space of silence. Helen spoke again.

"She'll have hidden it, they may never find it. I don't suppose they'll think we've got anything to do with it, if they do. And if they ask, we just have to do what we did today. Play dumb, all smarmy. Easy enough, they go for it every time."

"Made me nervous," said Patricia, "those policemen did." She looked upset still.

"Yes—and you showed it."

"I couldn't help it." The glasses were misting again. She took them off, for polishing with her hankie.

"Oh well—it didn't do any harm."

"She wouldn't have been pushed in or anything, would she?" said Angela. "She didn't go there to meet somebody, he didn't push her in?"

"Don't be a wally," Helen snapped. "Why would anybody want to push her in?"

They walked on.


Paul Ross turned out to be a slight lad with a lantern jaw, a pale face, and a guarded manner. Not hostile, toward the policemen, at any rate; but withdrawn, chill, unsmiling. Not, the policemen thought at once, at all the sort of lad you would have expected to be boyfriend to Deborah Hollowbone.

Even lumbered with a name like Hollowbone, a girl so pretty must have a wide choice, with more prepossessing young lechers panting to be up and doing.

They had waited in the car, parked on the opposite side of the road from the quite good detached house in which he lived with his parents and a younger sister—one of the older houses that were all that stood here until they built the new estate all around—and when they saw him come home they crossed the road and set the door chime tinkling.

His white face turned even paler when he heard why they were here, and muscles appeared tightened into little knots at the hinge of the lantern jaw. Obviously, news of the girl's death had not spread all over the town as yet. The local evening paper would be carrying it in the later edition, but this would not be on the street corners until half-past four, or stuffed through letter boxes later. The lad almost reeled when he was told, in the neat living room.

They asked the set questions, having no others to ask. No, he said, he did not see her last night. He saw her the night before. Their next date was for tomorrow. A disco. No, he had no idea why she should walk home through the woods. Routine questions and the expected answers, made with a blank, guarded stiffness not uncommon in adolescents faced with adult probing. Not uncommon, too, in people hit by sudden shock. They thanked him when they left, for his cooperation; thanked his mother—his father was at work—and went back to the car. Sergeant Wammo said as they crossed the road,

"Funny little bugger. Funny-peculiar."

"Mm. Common enough type. They become rating officers, work for the DHSS."

"Think he was knocking her off?"

"Could be. Somebody was."

"Can't see him all panting with passion."

"Never know, do you? They're all randy little sods, at that age. He was in shock."

"Talking of randy—I could teach that little blond one a thing or two. Cor!" The blond one must have been Helen. Angela was a brunette, and with Patricia it hardly mattered.

"You're turning into a dirty old man, mate, you know that?"

"I *am* one. It's come on me prematurely."

"Roll on Christmas," said Inspector Parsons, "I'll buy you a dirty raincoat."

They finished the day's work. Nowhere left to go, except back to the station. Nothing left to do after a brief call upon the Assistant Chief Constable, to tell him they were no nearer to establishing whether they were looking at an accidental death or a matter of murder. He was not perturbed, he broke none of their bones. An Assistant Chief Constable has many pots scattered about, some at simmer, some spitting fat, others bubbling up and over all at once. And he knows his men, he knows the brain will not stop working when the body walks out through the door. He knows, too, from his own experience, the value of the odd unexpected evening at home, as counter to the stresses implicit in a married copper's domestic life.

So he said, Go home. Give the wife a treat. Only don't take her to the pictures, or for a run in the country. Do it at home, within reach of the telephone. Something may just come up.

All quite normal. Tomorrow was Pete Parsons' rest day. Whether he took it or deferred it was up to him. There's a trouble, you see—very, very rarely does a working detective manage to enjoy a rest day plannned ahead. Something always comes up, if he tries to stick to the rota. So he is inclined to forgo them, in favor of snatching the odd untrammeled day as it appears. When it comes, because he has nothing planned, he tends to prune roses; especially when somewhere in the offing is murder. He won't go far from that.

Suzie Parsons (née Ferngrot) understood these things well. And she knew how to snatch for herself. So after dinner, when in answer to her question he said he didn't know yet, he might have to hold the rest day, she said, "Well—if we're not going to get our lie-in, we'd better have an early night."

He grinned. "What for?"

"Well," she said, "there's nothing on the telly."

When they were through with what they went to bed for, descending sweetly from pink clouds with warm nakedness intertwined, she spoke sleepily.

"Do you think old Wellborn-Davit's hair is real?"

"Real?" He was a little behind her in the descent. His mind, still drifting, took in the words only vaguely.

"We always said it was a wig."

"Could be." He moved a lazy hand, to stroke her undoubtedly genuine hair.

"What were they like, the kid's friends?"

"Like? Oh—all right. Nothing special. Nice girls."

"There are no nice girls."

"That's a bit sweeping." Lazy talk. Lovers' talk.

"You never went to a girls' school."

"True," he said. "Very true, that is."

"Hotbeds, they are. Sex-mad. Bitchery—bullying—crawling—the lot."

"You get bullying in boys' schools."

"Not so subtle, though. Horrible little monsters, girls are."

"You were a girl."

"I was the exception. Mmm—that's nice. Mmm—mmm—that's *nice*."

# ·5·

He decided to take the rest day. That he would not get it was something he could hardly know in advance when he awoke with a warm wife breathing in his arms on a morning glowing gold through the dawn curtains. It was so comfortable here, and the act of love with a loved woman followed by the night of peaceful sleep that succeeds it when it is done as it deserves to be done cleans a man's soul right out. He awakes gladly, and is proud to have hair on his chest. He kissed her, whispering,

"You awake?"

"Mm?" She opened her eyes and smiled to find him looking down at her. "Oh—it's you."

"There'll be trouble if it's not," he said. Very lucky, he was. She wore her hair short, and a natural wave meant that he was never clonked with curlers when her head should have come to nestle quietly between his cheek and his shoulder, or when she turned over suddenly. Nor did she come to bed like a pound of dripping, covered in Lardy-Creme.

The truth about Suzie: She loved the whole business of love; and whether by intelligence or sensualist's instinct, she knew that beauty comes not from bottles, but from loving and the overwhelming friction between loving genitals, lovingly combined. So, especially after loving, she even looked good in the mornings, with her hair tousled curly and her soft, curving lips and the hallo-my-love look in her eyes.

"Just thought I'd tell you," he said. "I'm taking the rest day."

"Oh, *good*." Her smile was a delight to him. Happy the man who looks at his morning wife and can love her. Happy the wife who can look without a shudder at him, whiskers and all. "Are we going out?"

"Shouldn't be suprised. After I've rung the station." A copper knows that if nobody rang him in the night, nothing is happening now, and—it is strange, this, but it is so—nothing is very likely to happen, probably until tonight. But if a case is brewing, should he take time off he must let the station know where he is going, and how they can contact him. And he—she—they—must be ready to cut the expedition short.

"Better get up and do it, then," she said.

"I'm not stirring from this bed," he said, "until I've had a cuppa."

Good for him. No hurry, and she always did bring him a cup of tea on his rest days. One of her little statements, to the effect that she thought the world of him. All these tiny things do combine to encourage the growth of hair on a man and his necessary ego.

Now this is when she *was* beautiful: when she got out of bed naked. It does seem an awful shame that they had no children. Never mind, they were happy enough. He watched with appreciation as she donned her dressing gown and sipped with appreciation when she brought his tea. Then, knowing she was under the shower, he joined her, and they teased each other a little with hands and soap. And then they had a good breakfast. The radio was on, tuned to the local station because this is the one that will tell you more of what you need to know. Nothing was said on the news about the dead girl. Nothing at all, she was old hat by now. Ah, the pity of it. A body as beautiful, as capable of splendid giving and taking as was Suzie, a potential as high, even if few people ever attain it. All dead. All cold without the living breath. All wasted.

They would go on the river. In a rowing boat. Mustn't waste this last spell of sunny weather. They would lunch at the Cocky Pheasant—somebody, surely, manipulated that name? It must have started out as the Cock Pheasant, which is a pleasant if tarted riverside pub where they serve good beers kept in wood and a famous pie. You can eat it in a window seat, if you are lucky and avoid weekends, overlooking the quite green water and the moss-gray bridge and all the lovely wooded country.

There are some who say the human body, male or female, is more erotic clothed than unclothed. Be they right or wrong—and it must depend on the body or bodies—these two made a pleasing sight, either way. She knew how to dress him as well as she knew how to dress herself. What holds true in bed holds true out of it: A thing done lovingly is a thing done well. By the time they were ready to go, you would never have believed that this was a copper and his wife. And then the bloody phone rang, when they were almost at the door. All he had left to do was make his call to the station, on the way out. Forthwith, she said, "Sod it."

He stepped aside, in the hall. Picked up the phone. Said, "Yes? Yes. Oh—hello, Wammo. Uh-huh. Mm. Yeah. Right. Right." Then he put the phone down and said, "Wouldn't you bloody know it? Wouldn't you just bloody know it?"

She cast away the plaited straw bag containing a trifle of makeup, a novel in case she felt like reading, her dark glasses, and the odds and ends without which no woman must stir from home. It thunked against the wallpaper and slid down, leaving a small scag that would call for Polyfix, the Better Wallpaper Paste. "Sod it, sod it, sod it," she said.

\* \* \*

He was at the station within ten minutes, knocking on the door behind which, the desk sergeant told him, he would find Wammo Wimbush. He did not wait for invitation before entering, because few people do things in police station interview rooms of which they would have been ashamed to be caught in the middle. Naughty things have been done—bribes passed, dates made for sex later, to get a run-in daisy off the hook and back on the beat. Things like that. After all, it was an old station, matured in grief and sin. You could hardly expect that over the thick part of a century, not one single copper bent. But such naughtiness is rare.

Wammo Wimbush was innocently engaged, chatting with two people in the ugly room. They looked stressed still, but less shrunken by grief today. Pete Parsons smiled at them all as he came in, very smart and alert-looking in his fawn slacks and the brown-mixture sports jacket snapped up by Suzie in the sale at Tweedledum Tweeds (London and Bradford). "Good morning, Mr. Hollowbone—Mrs. Hollowbone," he said. "Morning, Sergeant."

They all made some sort of good-morning noise, and Wammo Wimbush nodded toward the table. "In the box."

The inspector crossed, to raise the lid of a metal box that once held biscuits. The contents glittered. He lifted out a bracelet in gold—a good-looking necklace—a delicate watch, the golden wristband set with what sparkled like diamonds. Several other pieces were in there—brooches, rings, a second shimmering necklace. He said,

"You found them in her room?"

Mr. Hollowbone replied. "Just now. Well—early, really—we didn't sleep much—Ethel—my wife—went in to clean her—Debbie's—room a little. Straighten it up, you know what girls are. It was under the bed."

"You hadn't seen it before?"

"We never went into her room." Mrs. Hollowbone spoke up. "She is—was—old enough for—privacy. I'd just poke my head in sometimes. When she was in there. Just to see—"

"What sort of state it was in," said Mr. Hollowbone. "You have to watch them a little. You know how they are. But now . . ." His voice trailed off. His wife said, almost apologetically,

"I thought I'd just—tidy it up. Put things away. You know."

The sergeant certainly knew. He had these two sisters of his own, he remembered the early teens: the clothes pulled off and dropped, the hastily tugged-together bedclothes with counterpanes left awry, the perfumed bottles and tins of talc left uncapped on a dressing table marked with smears of the powder. The inspector had no sisters, but he remembered his own room. He said,

"And they're not fake?"

"The mounts and things are hallmarked," said Mr. Hollowbone. "The jewels—no. No, they're not fakes. I know a bit about these things."

"My husband used to work in a jeweler's," Mrs. Hollowbone explained. "Before he went to the Gas Board, of course."

"Did you ever see her wearing any of them?"

"No," they said; and Mrs. Hollowbone added, "She used to wear paste things—fashion jewelry—when she went out dancing or—out. And a silver identity bracelet we gave her for Christmas. They're in her drawer."

"Perhaps we should have brought them," said the husband. They had the close-cued speech pattern often found in people long fond of each other.

"It doesn't matter." The inspector was looking for hallmarks. They were there, all right. "Could she have saved up for them?" Because in these days, such things are possible. Some children get ridiculous pocket money, and they do not necessarily spend it on crisps and sweeties. Not all of it. They'd grow fat as butterballs and their teeth would be little brown stumps.

"No. Not her pocket money, we only give her—gave her—two pounds a week. And she spent that."

"She didn't have a Saturday job?"

Mrs. Hollowbone answered. "She was studying for her A-levels."

Mr. Hollowbone: "She had a lot of homework." Silence for a moment, while the policeman studied another piece. He added, "We thought we'd better bring them in. To you."

"I'm glad you did." Even though you've buggered my day. "Do you think she was looking after them for somebody? A friend?"

To Sergeant Wimbush, if not to the parents, the implication was obvious. All day and every day, people are telling the courts they were looking after things for a friend. Very often they speak the truth. It doesn't alter the fact that the goodies are bent.

A burgling boyfriend? The chilly lad? Somebody else? Shoplifting expedition? Who really knows what their children are up to? Especially parents like these seemed to be, trusting and honest enough to have brought this lot straight in, instead of hanging on and holding it, if only to divert any hint of funny business from their dead daughter. They seemed the archetypal innocents, the lady saying,

"None of her friends has got any money. They're all at school."

Apart from the ones, the sergeant thought, that you don't know about, met in discos and the like. Pete Parsons was saying:

"Well—we'll look into it, if that's all right with you. We'll hang on to the things for now; if you'll go with Sergeant Wimbush, he'll make out a list and give you a receipt. When

you've done that, we'll have Inspector Bramall take a look."
Inspector Bramall specialized in jewelery, antiques, things of
like nature. Very useful man—he'd be able to estimate the
value, find out from the hallmarks who manufactured them.
First step on the way to who sold them, in what shop or shops
and to whom. If they were nicked, he might know where from
and who did it.

Sergeant Wimbush picked up the tin box and the inspector spoke again, assiduously nurturing public relations as the
parents moved. "We appreciate your cooperation. Our job would
be a lot easier if everybody showed the same public spirit."

Don't overdo it, Dad, the sergeant thought. Mrs. Hollowbone turned, just short of the door. There were tears in her
eyes, suddenly. "We are not altogether convinced that somebody didn't push her in," she said.

A pause. Quite pregnant. The inspector spoke. "What
makes you say that?"

"Why should she be jumping about at Lovers' Leap?"
said Mrs. Hollowbone. "She wasn't that sort of girl." And the
tears overflowed, running down her cheeks.


Inspector Bramall had in his office all sorts of reference books,
old files, new files, packets of photos, and losers' descriptions of
valuable items stolen, many of them long ago and never traced.
Another policeman who had grown his job into a hobby. It took
him no time at all to deal with the hallmarks, scowling at them
with a jeweler's glass stuck in his eye and identifying the manufacturers from one of those books. Sergeant Wammo Wimbush noted the names and addresses, because these people
must now be contacted, asked whom they supplied. They
would give the names of middlemen, who must also be con-

tacted; and so on through to the retail trade. Not too onerous a task; the retailers would be located somewhere in the area, most like. Ignore the rest of the country. Ten minutes among his files convinced the inspector that the baubles were not known as stolen, and when asked to estimate value, he said,

"Well—not a great deal. Nothing outstanding here. I'd give you—what?—eight hundred quid for the lot. A thousand would be top whack."

"It's all kosher, though, is it?"

"Oh yes. Yes, it's kosher all right. Pretty, some of it, there's many have spread their legs for less. Not the ones with the mink coats, though."

"Thanks, Harry," said Pete Parsons. "Keep your hand on your halfpenny."

"At my age," said Inspector Bramall, "what else is there to do?"

And this is how policemen of respectable rank talk to each other, out of the public ear. Well, perhaps it is as well they let it all out. It keeps their lavatories free from graffiti.

Next step: work the Assistant Chief Constable into the frame. They went upstairs, Pete Parsons and Wammo Wimbush, carrying the tin box. The ACC said what they knew he would.

"Get them all photographed, find out where she bought them. Had she got a car?"

"No, sir."

"Shouldn't be far away, then. Got a photo of the girl?" They'd need one, to aid the memories of shop assistants.

"Not yet," Pete Parsons told him. "We haven't needed it until now. I'll send a car up, get one from the parents."

"Do that. All right, gentlemen, thank you. You're looking very smart, Mr. Parsons."

"Rest day, sir. I was just going to take the wife for a run in the country."

"Run in the country, eh? Nothing like it, for holding the weight down. Keep me in the picture."

No word of commiseration, no nod of approval for a man who just gave up his rest day. But there would have been a blistering rocket if he hadn't, and an indelible mark on the record.

Down the stairs again, back to the hoi polloi, where Sergeant Wimbush peeled off toward the photo lab and Pete Parsons to his office and the telephone, armed with the list of manufacturers.

The photographic laboratories in police stations are highly organized. "Laboratory" is a high-flown designation for what is, except in city headquarters, usually not much more than a darkroom staffed by two, perhaps three men, who do in truth no more than a press agency does all day long. A press agency is also highly organized, and both can, when they must, photograph, develop, print (using a glass plate, which goes wet into the enlarger), and supply copies, very nearly dried, in the time it takes to smoke half a cigarette as you wait in the annex where the cameras are kept, and printing frames, and the rotary drier, and a guillotine for trimming. Even a number of articles can be covered in remarkably quick time, using two or three upright copying cameras. Neither police nor press need or want tricky lighting effects and painstaking work with retouching brush and the spray gun. What they like is a good, plain record, sharp in every detail. And invariably, they want it *now*.

Sergeant Wimbush very nearly got it. He was in the inspector's office with his tin box and several neat envelopes containing prints before the car diverted to the Hollowbone house had arrived with another little copying job for the photo lads. That's quick work, the portrait of young Deborah was brought in while he waited for Pete Parsons to finish with his phone calling. Pete signaled acknowledgment to the squad car men who brought it, and carried on talking while the man laid the photo before him and tramped out.

"Yes. Well—it shouldn't be late. Mm. Yes—well, so did I."

A feminine dwarf gabbled in the receiver. That'll be the wife, Sergeant Wimbush told himself. He could not hear what she was saying, but then he didn't need to. He had one of his own, and many a lost rest day.

In fact, she was making no fuss. The girl who marries a detective accepts the result of so foolish an action, or she leaves him; and she had no intention of doing that. At least he rang. Some vanish for days and never get round to it; all their wives hear of them is what they read in the papers. Mind you, she was kicking a little, for form's sake.

"It's going to cost you," she was saying, in that tinny, tiny squawk. "Right at the door, *right* at the flaming door. And off he went like a rabbit."

"I'll take you to the Bahamas," he said. "Annual leave."

"No, you won't, some daft bugger will get murdered. Just don't expect any of the you-know-what for a week. I'm doing a Lysistrata."

There was no way he could answer that, with Sergeant Wimbush hovering. "Wammo's here."

"Ah. Did he hear?"

"I don't think so. Shall I ask?"

"No. Just say hallo for me. And tell him to give Dot my love. So what time do I expect you?"

"Soon as I can make it. We're only going round the jewelers' shops, they close at five-thirty. About six."

"Bring me back a tiara. And, lovie—mind how you go. Don't get run over. God bless."

"God bless." He hung up and spoke to the sergeant. "Suzie. Sends her love to Dot. Now—they the prints? Good. We're going for a cup of coffee while we wait for the lads to copy that"—he indicated the portrait photo, still in its frame— "then we're off to the city. Five shops, all supplied from one source." He picked up and studied the portrait briefly; handed it to his oppo. "That'll do nicely. Take it along, I'll order you a cuppa, fill you in in the canteen."


The drive to the city, nine miles away, was very pleasant on this fine morning, and lunch soon after they got there, guests of the city police, did nobody any immediate harm. The job itself imposed little strain. With only five addresses to visit, they did not separate but walked together around the city center. All the listed stores were here, in the modern shopping area close to where the buses come in from all the towns and villages for miles and miles around.

Two of the addresses yielded nothing. They were big department stores, too busy and impersonal to remember every customer who bought moderately priced jewelry in the jewelry department; but the other three were small specialized shops, and here they knew her. She had come in on Saturdays, at intervals over the past year. Smartly dressed—very mod. No, certainly they did not know she was a schoolgirl. But then, children develop so early these days, don't they. Some around here, you'd think they were thirty.

Yes, she always paid cash. Yes, they had records of the sales, naturally. But it would take a little time to go through the books.

No problem there. The policemen simply left the first

shop to sort the matter out while they visited the second and third; doing the same thing at each so that when they came back, the carbon-copy receipts were ready for them. The whole operation was finished comfortably by four o'clock, when they retired to a café for tea, sale dates, articles purchased, and amounts paid all entered in the sergeant's book. And the names she gave. At one shop, Miss D. Smith. At the second, Miss D. Jones. At the third, Miss D. Brown.

"Spread it about a bit, didn't she?" Wammo Wimbush said, stirring the tea and speaking through doughnut.

"She would, wouldn't she?" Pete was a toasted-cake man, and he did not have to go into details. Wammo knew as well as he what his book said, marrying all the dates together. Over the year, no one shop had been visited often enough for anybody there to wonder how a girl so young could be spending so much money. At one, when she bought the watch, she told the assistant it was for her mother's birthday. Two, three visits to a shop over a year will pass. Two, three visits to each of the three different shops, plus purchases at department stores, and you have a different picture. Especially if each shop knows her by a different name, none of them her own.

"Bent, then, our little birdie," Wammo said.

"Seems like it."

"Old Harry didn't do a bad estimate, did he? Thousand quid—he wasn't far out." Total in the book was nearly eleven hundred.

"He's a downy old bugger, is Harry. You've got jam on your chin. Wipe it off and I'll drive you home."


They did not, in fact, go directly home; home, in this instance, meaning the home station. On the way, they called again at that sad, raw house on the new estate. Father, mother, and young son were here, the man having taken the day off from work. Bereaved workers invariably do. The parents shared the answers to questions between them, son being seen but not heard.

It seemed that Deborah had been going to the city about once a month on a Saturday, to buy this jewelry a bit at a time over the past year. Did they know she was going there?

"She went more often than that. Saturdays—Wednesdays, sometimes. To look round the shops, and they'd go on Wednesdays to a disco."

"They?"

"She went with her friends. Sometimes all three of them, sometimes with Patricia only. And on Wednesdays with Paul, since she took up with him."

"Did her pocket money stretch to that, then? Two pounds doesn't go far these days."

"Well—two pounds was the basic. We used to give her a bit more when she needed it, to cover fares, admission, things like that. Provided we knew who she was going with, and so long as she didn't come rolling home all hours. Not that she ever did. We do the same with Clifford. Don't we, Clifford?"

The boy confirmed that they did.

"And did she give anything—the watch, say—for a birthday present? To her mother?"

"How could she? She gave bath salts."

"What I'm saying is: Even with supplements, her pocket money would hardly stretch to—what does the book say, Sergeant?—eleven hundred pounds' worth of jewelry in a year. Would it?"

"Eleven hundred pounds?" Here Mrs. Hollowbone's

mouth fell open and she raised a hand to her bosom. Mr. Hollowbone merely nodded, as if the sum were no surprise. The boy Hollowbone carried on sticking together a plastic glue-it-yourself Cruise Missile kit. He was doing it on the living room table, spread with newspaper to guard against fallout.

"Eleven hundred pounds. And false names given—Smith; Jones; Brown."

"Good God," said Mr. Hollowbone; and Mrs. Hollowbone, faintly: "Never!"

"You will realize that this puts a rather peculiar complexion on your daughter's activities."

"What complexion?"

"We don't know, as yet. But we shall have to inquire into it."

"Yes. Yes, of course you will."

"You don't know of any other—friends?"

"No. Only the ones we've told you about."

"Yes. Right. Well—if you do think of anything—anything at all—you know my number. Thank you again for your cooperation."

Back to the car once more; where Sergeant Wimbush said, "They're clean."

"I never thought they weren't." If they were involved in any way, they'd hardly have brought the trinkets in, inviting investigation. So easy, to have vanished them.

"Where to now?"

"Back to the shack. Get this lot officially logged, tie everything up."

"What about her mates?" If they went with her to buy the stuff, they must have known something about it.

"School's out, it's six o'clock. They can wait till the morning. My bet is, she went shopping alone, said she was going with them to keep her parents happy. Let's face it—if she had that much money, she could have paid her own fares, nipped off on the quiet."

"Only if somebody saw her in the city and told Mum and Dad, they'd have started asking questions. But if she'd conned 'em for the fare, she'd already told 'em she was going there. So if she was reported as being on her tod, she just said her mates had all gone for a Jimmy, or something."

"Not just a pretty face, lad, are you?" Inspector Parsons was steering the car neatly toward the station by now. "And vulgar with it. Young ladies don't go for a Jimmy, they gently tinkle."

"Mine did," said Wammo. "I was always having to give 'em two-pee pieces."

"That was sheer excitement. Stirred a few in your time, I have no doubt."

"I had my moments," the sergeant said. "Tell you what—the way it looks to me, she was a crafty little bugger, our Debbie."

That, virtually, ended the day. The Assistant Chief Constable was long gone when they reached the station. Not worth ringing him at home, he would not be biting his nails longing to be told what his senior investigators had been up to. So Pete rang his wife instead—Wammo was one who never bothered, because he didn't like his very much—to tell her he would be home in about fifteen minutes; as he was, having used five of them in linking up photos of the trinkets traced with place of purchase, prices paid, and date of visit.

An easy task, done already in the shops and so calling only for a few whacks on the stapling machine. And the statutory booking, which the inspector left to Wammo. What are minions for, if not to crouch cursing over typewriters and to see that goodies go into the safe for the night? Not that police stations feature high on the list of places popular for burglarious creeping, but even policemen have been known to go sticky-fingered.

They actually did get to the Cocky Pheasant, Pete Parsons and Suzie; but for dinner instead of lunch. He took it in a dark and sober suit, she in a yellow shimmering dress that she made herself, although you would never have suspected. He bought a better bottle of wine and she had out-of-season strawberries to make up for the lost day. And when they got home, nourished well on steak with salad on the side, they made love again.

And so they, along with all right-thinking lovers in the Western hemisphere, were sleeping peacefully in each other's arms when a Ford truck without lights crept along the school drive on the side not overlooked by houses, pushed by three herberts who had no desire to advertise by engine noise; and who, as soon as they had stopped it in the shadows, set about robbing the school.

## ·6·

A school in this age of fish fingers and the microchip is no mere repository for chalk sticks, scagged desks, scabby inkwells, and the spare teeth of long-dead pedants lurking undiscovered in unopenable drawers. On the contrary, it is a veritable goodie-trove stacked with computers for teaching tomorrow's citizens how to compute; with calculators to save wearing out valuable young brains and fingers upon the adding up; with television sets and video machines, complete with tapes. Recording equipment too.

Schools with music departments have record players, nicely portable musical instruments. Domestic Science departments contain expensive sewing machines. Cookery students study on great electric cookers that only need unplugging, the like of which they will never see again once they leave and marry and settle in a semi-det. Biology labs yield microscopes, and even a couple of white mice to be whipped by married burglars and taken home for the kids.

And all very lightly guarded, if guarded at all. The head teacher will certainly not sit up all night with bolting eyes and a shotgun, starting at every shadow. After all, it is only rate-payers' money.

Inspector Parsons and Sergeant Wimbush had no idea that this school had been broken and entered when they arrived there soon after nine on the following morning. The station knew; but they had not called in at the station. The senior man had collected the junior at his home, and they'd driven straight down. Wherefore, they were surprised to find one squad car, one unmarked but recognized dark saloon, one plumpish detective inspector called Charlie Begley, and Miss Wellborn-Davit grouped in the drive. The headmistress was talking, and seemed to be very upset. Charlie Begley was nodding his felt hat, gravely. The two detectives came out from their car and walked over.

"Good morning, Miss Wellborn-Davit," the inspector said. "Morning, Mr. Begley. What are you doing here?" In the station, he'd have said whop-ho, Charlie.

"Busted," said Charlie Begley. "Well busted." He did not need to add, in the night. Only the odd quick snatch happens in schools by day.

"How'd they do?"

"Nicely. Very nicely. Must have used a truck."

"Our beautiful computer," croaked Miss Wellborn-Davit, face upraised, white and tragic under the jet-black hair. She had to raise it, being so much shorter than they. "And we'd hardly had it a week."

The new-come policemen asked no further questions; not because they lacked a sudden rush of professional interest, but because there are ethics, and this was Charlie's job. Parsons said,

"Ah. How unfortunate. We seem to have picked a bad time. I was hoping for another chat with Deborah Hollowbone's friends. Would that be possible, do you think?"

"Is it important?" Wisps of the unlikely hair were coming adrift. Strange, how often this happens to a woman under stress. "They are overexcited already."

"It is, rather, I'm afraid."

The headmistress hesitated before turning away without

a word, making for the entrance door. The inspector moved off in her wake. Sergeant Wimbush lingered a moment, to murmur at Charlie Begley.

"You know who's caretaker here, don't you?"

A delicate nudge is not a question.

"Albert Fish," said Inspector Begley. "He's round the back, with Barry Fowler." Barry Fowler was his leg-sergeant. "That's where they got in, forced a door."

An unnecessary nudge. But as well to have delivered it. It was on the cards that Begley did not know. Albert might have failed to turn up this morning, the sergeant quite expected that he had. He said: "Well—have a happy day. Watch out for the jailbait." He followed his inspector and the little headmistress up the steps and into the building.

They saw the three girls this time in Miss Wellborn-Davit's office. Perhaps the music room had been cleared out last night. Piano and all? Possibly; it's surprising what three men and a truck can shift.

As before, the only one to show disturbance was the plump, bespectacled Patricia. Lovely Helen, pretty Angela stood before the policemen—nobody sat, this time. There were those good chairs, but not enough to go round; so everybody stayed on their feet—without betraying any of the overexcitement Miss Wellborn-Davit had promised. Again, the inspector spoke for the police, greeting the girls with his wide, warm smile.

"Good morning, lasses. Sorry to be bothering you again, just a few bits and pieces. Deborah—Miss Hollowbone. She went to the city quite often. I believe you used to go with her."

A pause before the answer, a glance between them. Quite normal, in young girls faced with unfamiliar authority, especially when it comes wrapped in a double weight of sexual potency. They seek reassurance from each other, they silently

sort out who will speak first. Invariably, they all begin together. The pretty ones did.

Yes, they went with her. Sometimes. Well—not very
often. About—well—every couple of months. No, not every
week. Well—maybe once a month, but they didn't think so.
No, neither of them kept a diary. No, they couldn't really
check. But it wasn't all that often.

"Try not to speak together, girls," Miss Wellborn-Davit
said. "No need to be nervous." And this from a woman almost
visibly twitching, with her hair slowly coming apart.

The inspector moved his smile to Patricia. "I believe
you went with her sometimes alone. Just the two of you."

"That's right," the girl replied.

"Speak up, Patricia," said Miss Wellborn-Davit.

"That's right." She added a few more decibels.

"Often?"

"No. Not very. Just—sometimes."

The policeman moved his smile again, to invite reply
from them all. One at a time or all together, he didn't mind at
all. He could stop them at will, sort it out if he needed to.
"What did you do, on these expeditions?"

Looked round the shops. Went to a café for tea. Went
disco-dancing, sometimes, in the evening.

"Shopping? Did you buy things?"

Sometimes. Well—a scarf. Jeans and things. Clothes,
mostly, when they or one of them needed something. Not
often.

"Jewelry? Did she buy jewelry, when you were with
her?"

Helen answered. "No. Well—costume jewelry. We all
did."

It was not the time to say: We have reason to believe
(police euphemism for "we know full well") that she bought

55

very much more than that. Cool and collected they may appear, but excitement come to break up the even tenor of routine must surely be leaping about already behind those toothsome bosoms. It showed in the one with rare abundance. No real need to blow them over the top, as adolescent girls blow so easily. No point in encouraging them to yap it all over the school—the town, come to that, through home-friends and parents—that something fishy attached to Deborah Hollowbone and her accidental death.

"Right. Thank you for your cooperation. That will be all."

"Back to your form room, girls," said Miss Wellborn-Davit. When the three had left her study, she croaked at the leading policeman: "Jewelry? Valuable jewelry?"

"Quite valuable," the inspector told her.

"But—where could she have got it from? They are not rich."

"We have reason to believe, from shops in the city."

"How very singular. Perhaps some of the other girls—"

"This is for your private ear only, madam." Not for public and through public, the press. Not yet.

The girls, to regain their form room, had to pass along the main corridor set with big uncurtained windows, overlooking the drive and the playing fields at the front of the school. Passing one of these windows, Patricia spoke almost in a squeak.

"They're taking Albert away. Look—they're taking Albert away."

"Shut up, you fool," hissed beautiful Helen.

"They know—they know about the jewelry—they know about—"

"Shut up—shut up—shut up!"

\* \* \*

Albert Fish was not arrested. He was asked to accompany the police to the station, they believing he might be able to assist them in their inquiries. How can a body refuse an invitation so delicately worded? They'll run him in anyway, if he does.

He was sitting in one of the interview rooms puffing jerkily on one of his hand-rolled cigarettes when Pete Parsons and Wammo Wimbush came back from the school. They knew he was in there—a word with Charlie Begley before they left had told them so—but they did not call in to see him. He wasn't their property, he belonged to Charlie, who would get stuck into him as soon as he was through with his probing around the point of entry, his listing of what was gone from the school. They walked right past the door on their way to the office where the safe is kept; and having collected their tin box, back to the stairs. Up which they went, to put the Old Man into the frame. Top dog in any police force is called the Old Man, as the officer leading any investigation is called the Guv'nor.

The Old Man, when he had mulled over the jewelry, came at once to the essential point. "So what we want to know is," he said, "where a schoolgirl of sixteen gets this kind of money." He glanced up at his two satellites, inviting participation.

Now there is one physical feature that all women hold in common. Well, there are several; but this is the one a policeman thinks of at once as source of almost all the trouble they cause or fall into and of any riches they may rapidly acquire. Probably the Assistant Chief Constable had it in mind already, in spite of its being widely acknowledged that he was a gentleman. Certainly Pete Parsons did. As for Wammo Wimbush, the feature and its supporting paraphernalia were seldom far from his thoughts. Closeted alone with the inspector, he would undoubtedly have worked it at once, very pithily; but up in this rarified atmosphere, matters are dealt with more delicately. So he held back while Parsons said,

"Racket of some kind? Drugs?"

"Drugs," said the ACC. "Could be. Is there any history of drugs, around the school?"

"None that we have on file, sir. Of course, it doesn't have to be around the school. She went to discos a lot." Considerable drugs trafficking takes place in discos and places where young people gather outside school hours.

"Are we covering the discos?"

"Getting on to it this morning, sir. Soon as we finish here."

"And none of this stuff is stolen."

"All legitimately purchased, sir. We have the receipts." So: no. In answer to your implied question: She was not minder for a burglar or burglars, nor was she herself a burglar.

Now Sergeant Wimbush, decencies observed, wheeled in the nitty-gritty. "Prostitution?" Downstairs, he would have said hawking it, or spreading 'em. But not up here.

"Mm," said the Old Man, letting a bracelet rotate in his fingers so that it sparkled in the light. "At sixteen? A schoolgirl?"

"We've had 'em in a lot younger."

"Hmm. What's the home background?" Because it is a fact that most youthful prostitution, like most young-male vandalism, apart from that perpetrated by rugby clubs and drunk drivers of Daddy's Rolls-Royce (which is put down to natural wild-oat sowing), is the fruit of a warped family tree.

"Very good, I think," said Pete Parsons. "Parents' marriage very stable, decent standard of living. Very respectable."

Wammo spoke again. "She'd have been only just fifteen, a year ago."

That needed no elaboration. If she had taken to the game, until her sixteenth birthday, each and every punter had been guilty of a serious criminal offense against her, and never mind how willing she was.

"Yes," said the Old Man. "I take your point."

"She could," Pete Parsons said, "have had a lover." A wealthy lover. Men by the time they are wealthy are usually aging; and old or aging men often like them young. Peter Abelard might well have gone to nick over Heloise. History records that she certainly could have tapped a thousand quid in trinkets out of him, no problem.

"If she was on the game," Wammo put in, "we ought to start looking about for a pudden-eater." Some simply cannot sustain the more fragrant dialogue proper to discourse with higher echelon. He meant pimp. A pudden-eater is a pimp.

"Our problem is," the ACC said, thinking that the wife wouldn't mind the gold watch, wouldn't mind it all, ". . . we still can't go flat out and treat it as murder per se."

"We can push it a bit harder, though, sir," said his young and highly regarded inspector. "If we start exploring the angles, something may turn up." Especially if a pimp was involved.

"Yes. True. Very true. Well—carry on, gentlemen. Keep me in the picture."


Down the stairs yet again went those burly policemen; and when they were passing the door behind which Albert Fish sat awaiting still the arrival of Detective Inspector Charlie Begley, they found coming down the passage toward them a Mr. Roger Dunbutt, a shortish man and verging on the fat. A man with hairy legs that rolled him when he hurried, as he seemed to be doing now.

"Hello, Roger," said Chief Inspector Parsons. "In to see Albert?"

A fair assumption. Mr. Dunbutt was Prisoners' After-Care, and Albert was a very good client. Not a spectacular one-off, but faithful over the years.

"Ah—Pete," the fattish man said. "Yes. Morning, Wammo. He gave me a tinkle."

Prisoners' After-Care people, clerks of the court, certain big-time and worthy villains are well enough respected by the police to be permitted first-name, even nickname terms. But not traffic wardens. And because Albert was not arrested, he couldn't be prevented from making phone calls at the tax-payers' expense, provided he did not start buzzing Sydney, Australia, or whispering long and dirty into the ear of any bird he might be collaring. An arrested man is permitted one call only. To his lawyer. If he is lucky.

"Pity about Albert," said Pete Parsons. "How long's he kept out of trouble?"

"Fourteen months, near enough," Mr. Dunbutt told him. "And I, for one, don't believe he's slid back now." Reproof. Merited, if the policeman's remark is construed as tinged with prejudgment. A touch pompous, but this is occupational self-preservation, in fattish officials who have to deal with the police and various other bureaucracies, on behalf of vulnerable malefactors. Either this, or they attempt to adopt police jargon and attitudes, neither of which they are equipped to sustain convincingly.

"How long's he been caretaker up at the school?"

"Since just after he came out. I got him the job. Well, Alderman Withers put a word in."

"Withers, eh? Good man to have on your side." Chairman of the Education Committee. Possible next town MP, it was said. Few said him nay, he had a lot of money.

"Yes, well, we have a few wires to pull, you know. Here and there."

Wammo Wimbush never could resist a good line when it was offered. With sex on his mind, he spoke up, grinning. "Talking of pulling the wire—wouldn't be up to a little pimping, would he, our Albert, in his spare time?"

The effect on Mr. Dunbutt was quite noticeable. His thick figure stiffened, his eyes popped, even his double chin quivered. "What right have you to say that?" he snapped.

"Sorry," said Wammo. "Just a gag. Only a gag."

"You've no right to say a thing like that. No right at all." And the man showed them his broad and umbraged back, turning aside to enter without knocking the room where Albert sat in company with a solid constable.

The policemen passed on. "You will do it, won't you?" said Mr. Parsons. "You ought to know better. Especially with do-gooders. Touchy little buggers, they are." Very quick to resent imputation against their old lags. And this one had the ear of Alderman Withers, together they had pulled Albert's wires.

"Christ," said Wammo, "it was only a bloody joke. Had it on my mind, that's all."

"What you have on your mind, son, should never see the light of day."

"Bollix," the sergeant said; and after twenty paces of silence, just before he turned in to the CID room while Inspector Parsons went on to his office: "It's a thought, though, isn't it? Old Albert. He's a canny old bugger."

"You're peeing in the wrong pot. Never touched it, has he?"

"Always a first time."

"Knock it over. If he's clean on the break and enter, he'll be clean all the way round. If he's not—and I think he is—he'd hardly want to call attention to himself if he was puddening on the side, would he? Not for the sake of what's in a school."

"Charlie says they got away with a fair old bundle."

"Yeah. But it's P.D. for Albert, if he comes up again."

P.D. is Preventive Detention. They give it in the end to habitual criminals. Twelve years at least.

Inspector Charlie Begley reminded Albert of this a little later. He arrived with his Sergeant Barry Fowler soon after Mr. Dunbutt entered the room where your man sat, and was rather annoyed to find that Mr. Dunbutt had asked the guarding constable to leave him and his old client to enjoy a private chat, and that the constable had done so and was standing in the passage outside the door. Policemen do not like to have their interviewees chatted before they themselves can get at them, particularly when the chat is with somebody holding however minor clout, undoubtedly there as support and probably watcher ready to pounce on deviation from Judges' Rules. These are the commandments strict adherence to which would castrate the police entirely, and reinvest power in the lap of the criminal classes. Mind you, they also prevent the occasional fit-up, and the odd cocky and obdurate interviewee's getting his head bashed in at the end of a long, hard day-and-nighter.

Inspector Begley, then, wore the face of stern displeasure when he suggested that Mr. Dunbutt leave; which he did quite readily. There was a phone call he needed to make. From a call box, on the way back to his office. So there were Inspector Begley and Sergeant Fowler, alone with Albert Fish; into whom they fairly pitched. As hard as they dared, bearing in mind the fact that Albert was no mug, he knew all about Judges' Rules and how to say in court that he had been subjected to cruel abuse and malodorous practices.

Albert's fingerprints were on the broken door. Of course

they were. As he said, they were bound to be, he used that door and every other in the course of his duties. They'd find his dabs everywhere, if they cared to look. No, he said, he wasn't surprised that his were the only ones—whoever knocked it over would wear gloves, wouldn't they? Diabolical liberty, he said it was, trying to fit it on him just because he'd done his bit of bird.

The policemen knew all about gloves, they privately knew that it would have been much more telling had Albert's prints not been scattered about, on the doorjamb and around the knob. They knew they had insufficient grounds for packing him into a cell, and as seasoned men they knew that in a case like this it is often better to let the suspect go. Put a discreet tail on him, see what he does and whom he meets. That way, you often net a whole gang. So Sergeant Fowler slipped away to arrange the tail, at a wink from Inspector Begley; who entertained Albert for five minutes more, using the constable called in from the passage as witness that he was wielding no rubber truncheon, before he said,

"All right, Albert. Hop it."

"I should bleedin' think so," Albert said. "Diabolical liberty, this is, Mr. Begley. I warned 'em long ago they'd get done, all that gear left hanging about like that. You can't lumber me with it; I'm clean."

"I hope so, Albert," said Inspector Begley. "You're just about due P.D. I'll walk you to the door."

He said this, and escorted Albert as far as the front steps, not from love of the man's company or from ingrained courtesy, but because however implicit his faith in his long-term junior partner, it is well for the senior man to see for himself that everything is as it should be. As a matter of routine, and to further unsettle him, he told Albert at the steps to keep himself available because no doubt they'd want to see him again; and he waited when the old lag was at road level and walking away, just to be sure that the man leaning against the wall along the street and reading a newspaper really was going to fold it, put it under his arm, and fall in behind at a sensible distance. Then he turned back into the building, not knowing that the next time any policeman looked upon poor Albert, he would be dead. Apart from the man on tail, of course.

# ·7·

By the time Albert left the station, Chief Inspector Parsons had sent two men off armed with copies of Deborah Hollowbone's portrait, to work over all the discos in town. On the wire was a further copy, and a request to the city police that they do similar, with the places she was known to have frequented there. Now he sat in his office, dredging up possibilities with Sergeant Wimbush, who said,

"Tell you what might be an idea. See her doctor."

"Doctor?" said Pete Parsons, absently. His mind was moving along a different track.

"He may have put her on the pill. Some of 'em do it nowadays without telling the parents."

"That's a point." The mind came back. Not urgently and quite easily. It hadn't been far away.

"If he did, he might know who was screwing her."

"Why would she tell him?"

"Didn't say he would, said he might. Doctors get to know a lot of things."

"Won't always spill 'em, though, will they?" Awkward buggers, they can be. It's all to do with privacy, sacred trust, and the Hippocratic oath.

"Worth a go. We might at least find out how long she was at it."

"If your brains were in your feet, son, I wouldn't want to be in your shoes."

An odd line. Sergeant Wimbush said, "What does that mean?"

"I don't know, I just thought of it. What's the Hollowbone number?" Mr. Parsons reached for the telephone, while the sergeant referred to his little black book.

One thing both men were very sure of: that parents so obviously decent and socially docile, kept in ignorance of a large and shady area in the life of a schoolgirl daughter only just come to the age of consent, would know nothing whatever about her sex life. Sexual activity is the thing above all that children hide from such parents, who prefer to believe that they have quashed the deplorable thing once they have smacked away the genital-caressing hand in its infancy. Certainly, these parents would not have condoned use of the pill, dating from soon after the girl's fifteenth birthday. Sooner than that, probably—who knew when she began?

Equally certainly, it would loom large in their thinking if they knew about it and tolerated it as a lesser evil than pregnancy. If, in fact, they knew their daughter was at it with right good will, as the pathologist said she must have been. And they would have mentioned it, as possible source of her jewelry, possible cause of her death. We often warned her—she wouldn't listen. . . . Something like that.

Of course, they may have known and kept silent to preserve the unspotted name. But the policemen didn't believe this. Parents not satisfied that their child died by accident are, almost without exception, keen to advance reasons why it wouldn't be so. So when Inspector Parsons raised Mrs. Hollowbone, and she asked why he wanted the name of the family doctor, he did not charge in and say: Because we think she may have been on the game, our doctor says the welt was almost worn off, we think she may have earned the jewelry on her back or, given the suppleness of youth and a certain talent, by covering the fifty-seven positions. No point in piling distress upon distress. He said merely,

"It's a routine part of our normal inquiries, Mrs. Hollowbone. We have to cover everybody who had any sort of relationship with the—er—subject."

Mrs. Hollowbone was willing to believe. Further indication that she knew nothing about it, if her daughter was on the pill. The family doctor would be the one to prescribe it. "I don't see how the doctor can help you," she said. "He only saw her when she had flu, something like that. Swollen glands."

"Even so, may I have his name and address?"

She supplied them. He thanked her, broke the connection with his finger, waggled the support up and down, and said to the WPC on the switchboard, when she came: "Phone number, love. Dr. Hackett, 15 Bishop's Close."

The doctor was a Scot, by the rolling of his voice, and a cautious one. He would not say a word until he had rung the inspector back, to verify that he was who he claimed to be and speaking from the police station. Even then, he was very terse and clipped; until Pete asked whether he'd prescribed the pill for her, when he exploded.

"Cairtainly not. The gairl wiz nae mair than a wee bairn."

"She was sixteen, Doctor. A lot of them start younger than that."

"Aye, soo they tull me. But they dinna geit nae help frae me."

One of the old school, well capable of savaging a haggis. "Did she ever ask you for it?"

"She did not. She'd hae got a skelping if she had. Ah havenae seen her for a year or mair."

"Thank you, Doctor. Are you a Catholic, by any chance?"

"A mon may hae his prunciples weeoot being Papist. Noo, if ye'll excuse me, I hae ma buziness to atteind tae." Click.

Pete Parsons replaced his phone. "Wonderful doctors, the Scots," he said. "Saw your leg off and think nothing of it. Clap a porridge poultice on the stump. There's a flaw in your reasoning. She wouldn't have gone to the family doctor."

"That's what they do," said Wammo Wimbush. "We have 'em in, sometimes. And they're always on about it in the papers, they go to the family doctor."

"Not that one, they don't. Ah well—we'd better follow it up. Get a few more prints run off, we'll send a couple of lads around. Four, if we can afford it. Cover all the doctors in town." No need to tell Wammo why the photographs were needed. If she went to another doctor, she'd probably have given a false name. Smith—Jones—Brown.

Through the day, men went round to the discos, town and city, knocking on the doors of proprietors who did not open until the evening. Others visited the doctors in town, one end to the other. Pete Parsons and Wammo Wimbush stayed in the station, catching up on paperwork relating to their general workload; until, after a canteen lunch, they visited several town discos where she was known, to follow up reports come in. No doctor at all claimed her. Complete blank, on that one.

Nor did the disco visits yield much fruit. Yes, they knew her. Came in sometimes with friends—by description, Patricia alone or the full trio from school—or with a lad; again by description, the pale and lanky Paul Ross. Well—she just did what they all do—drank Coke, hopped about. With anybody in particular? Well—they didn't take all that much notice of individual kids, so long as they behaved themselves. Well—they didn't much like coppers chivying about, but if they wanted to come back, talk to the kids—well—nothing they could do about it, really, was there?

While all these visiting policemen were going about their plodding business, hand bells rang all over the country, books were packed away, and the schools turned out. Those teachers ruled over by Miss Wellborn-Davit trailed off to the staff common room, looking for aspirin, the latest robbery gossip, and, with luck, a cup of soothing tea left in pot since break, lukewarm but better than nothing. They'd had a hard day, trying to pound education into adolescent girls gleefully excited by the break-in, and by the taking away in a squad car of Albert, the well-known caretaker. Eyes other than those of Helen and Angela and Patricia saw him go, and had no reason to button the lip. It was all over the school within minutes.

The girls left as they always left: in ones and twos and in little bunches, most of them scurrying round to where the break-in took place. They were shooed away by a constable prudently left there on guard. Not that there was much to guard; the investigating team had finished with it all and left, long ago. But as Miss Wellborn-Davit said, they didn't want three-hundred-odd girls rushing in and out, all bringing clues excitedly to Mr. Furmace. The science master, i/c microscopes. He now had no microscopes, but faith dies hard.

The Helen/Angela/Patricia consort did not join the rush. They had joined the lunchtime one that was frustrated by police and teachers acting together, but more for appearances' sake than from interest. They were mentally occupied with more personal matters. They walked down the drive together as usual, and their speaking was not meant for other ears. Patricia half-whispered,

"Perhaps it wasn't because of the robbery. Perhaps they took him about—"

"Don't be daft," said Angela. "It's about the robbery. He's the caretaker, isn't he? Well, then, they'll want him to—make a statement."

"Where is he, then? Why hasn't he come back? It wouldn't take all day."

"How do you know?" Pretty girls at the best of times use often a snappish tone toward these plain and comparatively dowdy friends, being somehow convinced that less attractive means more stupid. It was very apparent in Angie today.

"They're questioning him. I bet they think he did it."

"Of course he didn't do it. He wouldn't be such a wally, would he?"

"I didn't say he did it—I said they *think* he did it."

"*You'd* think anything. Even if they do, it doesn't affect us."

Helen spoke. "How do you know? You've never been questioned."

"I've seen it on telly, though, haven't I? *Everybody* knows. They browbeat you into confessing. There was a documentary last night about a man who confessed to a murder, and he's done five years and he didn't do it."

"Oh, belt up, Fats," said Helen. She turned to Angie. Most people called her Angie. "We're supposed to be going there tonight. Are we going?"

"I'm not," Patricia chimed in, promptly; and Angie:

"I'm laying off, until we've seen Albert."

They walked a little way in silence. Down by the gate, Helen said, "I think I'll go to the Blue Grotto, then. Coming?"

Angie saw the sense of it at once. She said yes. But Patricia said, "I'm not; I'm staying in."

Helen turned on her. "Your mum and dad'll wonder

why you're not going out." They had told their parents, all of them, that they would be going out this evening. Their jelly-friend was frightened; questioned at home, she might spill anything.

"I'll say I've got a headache. I'll go to bed."

It came as no blow to Sergeant Wimbush when, as they drove back to the station after their last disco visit, his superior officer said,

"Do you want to do the call-backs, then?"

He meant did the sergeant want to go again around the discos, and he was offering it as a courtesy. Since the introduction of overtime payment to CID officers—they never used to get a penny beyond what they could fiddle on expenses, though they toil nonstop for a week—evening work has increased enormously in popularity, and to heck with the wife. Let us be absolutely honest: It is by no means unknown in the periods of slack that do come sometimes, even to detectives, for a man or men to spend quiet afternoons poring over paper-work and making it look good, only to galvanize at five-thirty, and away to deal with suddenly urgent and vital matters that will provide employment in pubs and clubs until midnight. Temper the view, though: Much of their work is done by necessity in the evenings, and the pubs and clubs are where the villains gather.

They shared a good understanding, these two men. Wimbush knew that Inspector Parsons much preferred the company of his wife to slogging about the town all night, and having for many a year—nor was he alone in it—secretly coveted the inspector's wife, he quite saw the point. His own wife was presentable, you did not have to beg that people would not laugh when you introduced her; but somehow—. Well—frankly, he would sooner have the overtime. So he said, knowing that the job would not support two ranking officers,

"Yeah. All right, if you don't want it."

"If nothing comes up, I'll get another early evening, give Suzie a treat." (So would I, so would I! thought Wammo. It is probable that they were thinking along different lines.) "You should only need one man." No need to stay together, they could work one to each venue.

"Uh-huh."

"You know where I am, if you need me."

I know where I'd be, said the goat-bearded mind of Sergeant Wimbush. With the phone off the hook. "Right," said his mouth. "I'll see to it."

At six o'clock, give or take a little, Inspector Parsons arrived home, where he spent a pleasant evening in company with his very pleased wife. She had been into town, and came back with new videos from Robson's Video Hire. "Nasties?" he asked, with a horrible leer.

"*Sound of Music*," she told him. "And *Mary Poppins*."

"Well, they don't come any nastier," he said, "but I'd sooner have one where they eat babies."

They played with the video machine—she was only kidding, she knew what films he liked. A good Western, or anything with Henry Fonda—and went to bed early, at about the time when Albert died.


The Blue Grotto was the last place on Sergeant Wammo's list. It is a smallish place; you go down steps from the street to basement level. Some, with ready wit, call it the Blue Grotty, but this is hardly fair. It is clean enough, the decor passes, even looks attractive when the psychedelic lighting plays upon it. Be just, the very Paris nightclubs look utterly grotty by day. There is room to jig about in here, and a minuscule stage backed by lunatic-loud amplifiers with twittering lights before which a local youth with dreams sits, snapping fingers at a microphone, and bellows through it between records, so loud you cannot hear a blind word he is saying. All of this is what the kids like. And the police approve the place; it rarely gives them trouble.

When he entered, the colored lighting was bouncing off the mirror-ball above the jigging floor and the noise would have shattered a steelworker stone deaf from long exposure to roaring infernos. He looked from the elevation of two steps leading down from the entrance vestibule over a flock of cavorting youngsters indistinguishable from those in places already ticked off in his book; except that one of them was the beautiful Helen, and she was partnered by the lad Paul Ross.

He did not know them at first. For one thing, it is not easy to see who is who and with whom in that sort of lighting. For another, upper-form post-pubertals look so different out of school uniform. The girls suddenly, startlingly, are gone from pink bud to most decidedly fruit, and the boys could do worse than ask Father Christmas for a whisker-trimming set.

Helen wore a short, full skirt that showed generously her lovely slim legs when she meant to, and she meant to often. Those who do, in disco dance, have subtle hand-flicks and rotary steps to set things swinging. Above the skirt she had a white blouse, cut low and pulled down to off-the-shoulder. The lad wore jeans with a decent shirt, and seemed to experience no great pleasure from the dancing or his partner. His successively red, green, and blue face (it was his normal white, no doubt, but disco lighting does funny things to faces) was as lacking in animation, as deficient in joy, as when the policemen saw it at his home.

The proprietor, a husky man who acted as his own chucker-out, came to stand beside the sergeant. He nodded toward the couple. "Word with them two might help you, he was her stud." Had to shout to make it heard.

"Stud?"

"Well—I don't mean he was necessarily screwing her, we call 'em all studs, poor little bastards. Studs! Jesus Christ, look at 'em, half of 'em couldn't shag a paper bag. The other half probably do, to keep Mum's sheets clean. The chick was a mate of hers. So was that one." He nodded again, at another couple.

The male might have been a stud, he had the build and some of the necessary looks, if they carried over from this colored dimness into the harsh light of day. The female—it was not easy to see so far, but focusing upon one couple made identification possible—was Angela. In jeans of some superior sort, with a top rather less showy than that of lovely Helen, who saw the sergeant now.

She recognized him at once, and her supple undulating seemed to check for a moment; then she smiled. The Ross lad's face turned to find out at whom. He showed nothing at all when he saw the policeman. Nothing at all; he carried on without pause, without joy, without any discernible talent. Lumpish, his dancing was. And he a lanky lad. Wimbush smiled, and raised a greeting hand.

"So what are you going to do?" the proprietor was shouting. "Move among 'em asking if they knew the kid? Because you'll have a flipping job. She was often in—most of 'em are regulars—they *all* knew her."

"No—when this number finishes, I'll get on the mike. Just ask if any of 'em saw her the other afternoon. Take it from there." Nobody, he believed, would have seen her in any useful way. None of the kids in other places had. Still, it was all work, all solid overtime.

"You'll be lucky. You can't understand a word comes out of that bleeding thing. They never even listen to it."

"Why don't you buy a new one?"

"They like it. Keeps the noise level up. Besides, that silly young bastard'd blast the guts out of it first go. Roars into it like a bloody elephant."

"Get a new mike *and* a new DJ."

"They *all* do it. The kids like it. They like him, Christ knows why. They don't have to know what he says."

"What does he say?"

"Christ knows, you can't hear it." The proprietor grinned, waving a permissive hand. "Feel free. If you want a Coke after, I'll be behind the bar." No license, so nothing harder than Coke. Except what the kids smuggled in in flasks and wee bottles, as they will wherever they go.

The number finished. The DJ was in action before silence could fall, bellowing away with the mike so close to his lips that one small slip would have chipped his front teeth. Out of the speakers came the sort of raving jumble that used to be a feature in railway stations, and still does feature at sports meetings and wherever a speaker can be suspended from a tree or hung from a marquee, with a mike attached to be roared into. Sergeant Wimbush crossed the floor. He said to the lad, with a flash of ID card:

"Police, me old china. I'll just have a go on your yakking machine."

"I don't know about that," the lad said. They are very jealous of their prestigious position. Don't like other people fiddling with the gadgetry. "I make all the announcements."

"Move over, son."

The sergeant spoke his little piece, holding back from the mike so that some of the youngsters looked around, surprised at being addressed in plain English, quite intelligible. There was whispering out there on the floor; then two couples began to advance almost timorously, to where the man stood on the little platform. Helen and Paul Ross, Angela and her big stud stayed where they were, over by the steps leading up to the vestibule.

Nice-enough youngsters, those who approached; but since one lad believed he had seen Debbie way over on the other side of town, where she could not have been, and the other couple realized with confusion that they had the wrong day, no promising grist came to the sergeant's mill.

While he was speaking with them, most of the other kids shoved away up to the vestibule, where the Coke-and-crisp bar is, perhaps to escape the silence paining their cacophony-proofed ears. With them went Helen and Angela, who met in a relatively untenanted area by the lavatories, which are at the far end of the vestibule and well away from the bar. They could manage only a quick whisper; humanity in general tends to shove past into lavatories when it finds itself in proximity to them. Angie said,

"It's that sergeant, the one up at the school."

"I know," said Helen.

"What's he doing here? What's he asking about Debbie for?"

"I don't know."

That is all they could whisper. A whole party came whooping up to mill around, peeling off to enter the lavatories in ones and twos, the males left outside urging those within to hurry up, for Christ's sake, because they were bursting. The two girls moved on, joining a press of hot bodies at the bar. The vestibule is much more brightly lit than the dancing area, and people converging en bloc on the bar after a time of close-packed cavorting down there give off almost visible steam.

The proprietor does his best, but when everybody arrives like that in a mass, it takes a little time to get served if you are not first in the stampede. By the time the girls were equipped with a Coke each, the policeman was leaving. They came face-to-face with him as they approached the door leading back to the dim-lit dance floor.

He smiled widely upon them, the goat-beard of his mind sprouting additional whiskers. It was flourishing tonight, many of these little birdies would have—he told himself—pinned one on old No-Ball Johnson. No-Ball Johnson was a fast bowler in a local cricket team who unfortunately gathered the nickname by losing essential equipment when he impaled himself on spiked railings, bolting from a shop he'd been trying to rob. Wimbush said: "Ah—good evening."

"Good evening," the girls replied, speaking as politely as they did at school. Helen even bestowed her beautiful smile upon him. The goat-beard bristled and said *cor-r-r!*

"Having fun?" His eyes were seeing the pure glory of her neck, the subtle beauty of white bosom showing a mere soupçon of upper breast, the slimness of bare shoulders.

"Yes," they said.

"Good. Good. Working myself, or I'd ask you for a dance."

And now his brain realized a thing. There was a mark or something, above where a willowy-slender arm met her left shoulder. It looked like—makeup?

This is exactly what it was. Makeup, thickly applied; gone tacky from the heat, streaked by her—well, sweat (even lovely young girls sweat)—to reveal a little of what it was meant to hide.

"That'd be nice," she said, and realizing the direction of

his eyes, she raised her Coke-free hand. It came across her beautiful breasts to cover the spot; but not before his eyes and his mind focused together, and he said to himself: Somebody's sunk their teeth into her. That's a bloody great lovebite.

It was surprise, perhaps, that held him from questions. He had no right to ask any, of course, the girl was sixteen; but people usually answer quite meekly when a policeman speaks. Surprise, and a pang of disappointment, because every goatman with eyes slanting upon a tender young person sees in his fantasy himself as first and only one, teaching trembling innocence the things it didn't know and never dared to ask. He said,

"Well—enjoy yourselves." And he passed on, out into the night. This, too, was at about the time when Albert passed suddenly over.

# ·8·

Undoubtedly, somebody would have stumbled upon poor Albert long before had he not been tucked away in the back alley, where only dustbins go. He lived in a tall block of concrete apartments such as are crumbling and cracking all over the country, and he appeared to have fallen out of the window. Which should not have killed him, because he lived on the ground floor.

Sanitary operatives do not work at night. When they were dustmen they used to, but give a man a title like that and a yellow hat in place of his old cloth cap, and what does he do? He demands double time for tea breaks. Wherefore, town councils coax them to do a little work while the sun is well up, and they are back in the pub or in front of the telly before it sets. Even in winter.

The man tailing Albert—or, to be strictly accurate, the man who took over from that man—was called off at midnight; because to maintain watch all night is prohibitively expensive, and ties a man up; and any fool can spot a character hanging about all through the lamp-lit small hours. An early-shift man took up position in an unmarked car at 6 A.M. By which time, of course, Albert was stiffened into rigor mortis. He was dead even before the midnight man went home.

The first intimation to the police that he had perished came from one of these sanitary operatives at about eleven o'clock, when he went into that alley at the back of the flats, and came out to confer briefly with his mates, two of whom went in to have a look. After brief conference, the first man came directly over to the car in which the policeman sat and said, "'Morning, Guv. Excuse me, but we thought you ought to know. There's a body in that alley."

So much for discreet anonymity. And the copper was in plain clothes.



In view of his recent questioning of Albert, and the fact that he was the man who put the tail on, this case should have come directly to Inspector Charlie Begley. To higher up than he, of course, as head of the investigation; but when the parts were handed out, a heavy load should have come to him.

The reason why he was bypassed for the nonce is very simple: He was somewhere en route to Birmingham, where he would take charge of three herberts who could, he had reason to believe, help him in his inquiries, they having been apprehended in a plain van that hit a bollard. Glass tinkled, the bonnet bent upward, the back doors flew open; and there was a batch of expensive goodies, thought to have been stolen from the Queen Victoria School. They were unfortunate, these herberts, in that they were all sitting in the cab. The front doors jammed when the bonnet bent, and they couldn't get out.

A policeman rushing along a motorway is well beyond walkie-talkie range and out of station-radio contact. It is not easy, unless you arrange patrol-car interception, to reach him and turn him back. Wherefore, Inspector Begley and his leg-sergeant rushed on, and Chief Inspector Parsons stood in. You cannot leave a body lying about until one specific officer is free to deal with it. Especially when the body is that of an old friend. Well—say, customer.

The reason why Chief Inspector Parsons stood available was equally simple. He had nothing to do but the never-ending and heartily loathed paperwork. Wammo Wimbush was out, gone directly from his home this morning to deal with one of his other jobs, suddenly blown over. Had he snuffed out anything offering a lead last night, he would have reported it by telephone before leaving. He had not done so. The Deborah Hollowbone job was hanging fire, and Parsons was in his office with nothing to do. Nothing that he wanted to do.

When he heard that Albert was currently lying huddled among dustbins—and a thing like that is all over a police station in minutes—he went up to see the Assistant Chief Constable. The ACC agreed that, under the circumstances, he'd better go and have a look. He, the ACC, would sort out a superintendent to take the matter over, as per the book, should it turn out to be murder.

Because at this stage, of course, Albert had not been murdered. He was not even dead, officially. No body, however bloody or decomposed, is officially dead until a police doctor has declared it so.

Within ten minutes, Parsons was stepping from his car and making for the alleyway, nodding as he went past to a patrol car constable stationed at the entrance. He found the little fat doctor already there, rising from his kneeling position beside Albert, the tail-man standing by. "Morning, Doc," he said.

"Morning," said the doctor. "Not much doubt about this one. Back of his head stove in."

The inspector glanced up at the open window of Albert's flat. "Could he have done it falling out?"

"Nope. He'd have been unconscious, at least. Couldn't have turned himself over." He did not need to point out that Albert was lying face-down.

"Anybody touched him?" Because somebody might have

turned him. Not likely—people coming upon a supine figure tend to turn it from face down onto its back, not vice versa. But you have to ask.

The tail-man spoke up. "Only the doc. The dustmen are out in the street, if you want to have a word with them."

Pete knew this; he'd seen the dustcart and the four men standing with it. He said, "How come you're here?"

"I was supposed to be keeping tabs on him."

"Cocked that one up, son, didn't you?"

"I didn't come on till six." The policeman was a young one. He looked quite worried.

The inspector turned back to the doctor. "What time you reckon he died?"

"Impossible to tell. Rigor's well in evidence. Any time within the last twelve, fifteen hours. Or more. I'll know better when I've had him on the slab."

No need, between professionals, to hammer points. Rigor mortis is not, as the thriller reader is led to believe, a reliable guide to time of death. Twelve hours, more or less, elapse between its setting in and its beginning to wear off; and the more or less, even the time of onset, is affected by too many unstable elements. The entire process from stiffening to complete relaxation can take anything from thirty-six to forty-eight hours, and even this is not hard and fast. No pathologist uses it anymore to estimate time of death. They have better methods.

"Uh-huh." Pete bent over Albert. "Anything we should know about?"

"Only what you can see, so far as I can tell at this stage." Never a flat statement, always a qualification. And delivered in a tone of fussy irritation. Truly, a fat little pathologist can be a trial.

"Uh-huh." What Pete could see was very little. Unless

the back of the head is comprehensively bashed in, not much shows among the hair. He rose and said, "Poor old Albert. Now who'd do a thing like that? All right, Doc, thanks. We'll have him down to you as soon as the lads are finished. Do me a favor—tell the squad car lads, on your way out." They'd know what to do—radio to the station, bring out all those scruffy but clever specialist characters.

The doctor managed to make his bag snap irritably as he closed it. He then departed. Pete Parsons said to the tail-man,

"Don't have to ask if you saw anything."

"Nothing. Well—plenty of people coming out, going to work. Few women, off to the shops. Milkman—postman. Dustmen."

"Uh-huh." The picture was clear. "Who'd you take over from?"

"Nobody. Nobody here since midnight."

That picture, too, was clear. Bit of a cock-up, really; but then, every tail cannot be mounted with presumption of murder. Albert had never been more than a small-time thief. Even the school robbery was comparatively small-time, meriting no more than a small-time tail. No reason to believe he'd get himself knocked off.

"Where's his wife?"

"Wife?" Plainly, the lad didn't know he had one.

"Wife. Anybody told her?" To phrase it another way: How come she isn't here? She lived in the flat, surely? If he went through the window—if he wasn't done elsewhere and dumped in the alley—where was she, while it was being done? How come she didn't call the police?

"Well—no. Not that I know of."

"You haven't knocked on the door? Didn't send anybody up?"

"I couldn't leave him, could I? I was the only one here till the car arrived."

"How many entrances to these flats?"

"Well—I dunno. I only came on at six."

"Son," said Pete Parsons, "I don't think you're going to make Chief Constable."

"I'm resigning next week," the lad said. "Got a job with the Co-op."

"Go and do it now. Take one of the squad car boys. Knock on the door. If she's there and she doesn't seem to know, break it to her. Gently, don't just say, 'Oi, missus, your old man's had his head bashed in, down by the dustbins.' Off you go. And tell the other lad to radio the station. Sergeant Wimbush to contact me as soon as he gets back." The inspector looked up and around at the windows. Many of them, all the way up the tall building, showed heads, craned out and looking down. Friends and neighbors. All to be interviewed, no doubt.

Sergeant Wimbush got back to the station with a busted lip. The fool he went to fetch punched him in it, not realizing the explosive power of the sergeant's dreaded left hook. It took a long time to bring the silly fellow round, and they had to call a doctor to him when they had him laid out in a basement cell.

The sergeant was at the mirror in the CID room, where detectives who have any, comb their hair from time to time or writhe their lips back to inspect, those who have any, their teeth. He was dabbing soothing cream on the lip when Inspector Parsons' message reached him, and worrying a little. Hit a man too hard, ruck him up too much, you can find yourself in dead trouble. The message received, he cast aside cream and care and reached for his jacket. Before leaving, he did an intelligent thing.

He went to the files and abstracted the carbon-copy reports by the men who'd tailed Albert. Pete Parsons would want to read them. No point in his coming back here, when he could do it on the spot. A very good support man, this sergeant. He got himself a lift in the car of a specialist who was going down; and so was able to read through the reports en route. Now he could summarize immediately, should Pete require it.

By the time he arrived, Pete was standing by, watching the specialists going about their work of measuring, photographing, scraping up little bits of things and putting them into plastic bags. The ambulance and a string of cars stood at the curb, the alley entrance was roped across and guarded, various neighbors were grouped on the far side of the street. The squad car crew and the lad who arrived at six were already knocking on doors in the block of flats, asking questions. All was as it must be at the start of a murder inquiry. Full house-to-house teams would be arriving shortly. The sergeant stepped over the rope. Pete Parsons said as he approached,

"Hello, Wammo. Who did that to your lip?"

"Harry Barnet," said Wammo. "Jumped straight out of bed and belted me."

"Silly fellow." The inspector did not have to ask what happened to Harry Barnet. "Somebody seems to have done Albert."

"So I believe. Poor old sod; why would anybody do that? Albert was harmless." Nobody had told the sergeant the cause of Albert's death, but it was pretty obvious, seeing him lying there.

"The school job? Quarrel over the pickings?"

"Could be. Seems a bit extreme."

"May not have meant to kill him. Heat-of-the-moment job. The dustmen found him, thought he'd fallen out of the window."

"That wouldn't kill him; he lived on the ground floor."

"Might have been bashed inside. Trying to get out. Had the window up—*bam*—out he went."

"What about his wife? What's her name—Ellie?"

"She's away. Staying with her mother, the woman next door says. Went Tuesday, due back tomorrow. Bloody neighbors in these warrens know everything; we've even got the address. Derby."

Again, no need to elaborate. It's all routine. The Derby police would break the news to Mrs. Fish, and supply a car to bring her home. Wammo said, "What's it look like inside the flat?"

"Haven't been in"—and couldn't without authorization, until Mrs. Fish came home and unlocked—"but you can take a shufti through the window. No sign of struggle."

An Inspector Fitter came up. He said, "All right, Pete—we're finished. You can take him away."

Take him away? *Take* him away? Chief inspectors do not stagger out of alleys with rigor-mortised corpses draped across the shoulders. "Righto, Benny," said Pete Parsons. "Tell the ambulance wallys, will you?"

"What about a weapon?" asked Wammo. Because the bashing in of Albert's skull would not have been done with the clenched fist. "Would that be in there?" Thus, with tact, does junior rank convey to the senior a hint that the need to search for a murder weapon may justify immediate break and entry into private property.

Pete Parsons took the point quickly. He had already mulled it, in his mind. "That'll be up to Charlie. I'm only keeping the seat warm."

"Be an hour or two before he gets back." Wammo reached into his inside pocket; brought out the long buff envelope in which he carried the papers. "Albert bumph in here—surveillance reports. Thought you might want to look at 'em."

"Good lad." While Parsons lowered his head over the papers, the men from the police ambulance arrived to take Albert away. They carted him off between them with the black plastic sack draped over. He was too stiff to fold, and you have to fold them to get them inside. The inspector raised his eyes and said,

"Visited Alderman Withers."

"Yeah. And Roger Dunbutt."

"Whining about the school job, no doubt. Brutal and licentious constabulary."

"Never felt licentious about Albert, personally."

"Came back here, never went out again."

"Uh-huh."

The inspector refolded the forms and put them with the envelope into his own pocket. "Well—it'll all be down to Charlie."

It happened that he was wrong. It was not all down to Charlie. When they arrived back at the station, an item of news was just in.

It concerned Charlie. Detective Inspector Charlie Begley, who'd arrived in Birmingham with no more bother than the aggro implicit in arrival at any motor-age town: three times round the one-way system before you can find your way to anywhere, whether you want to go there or not. Together with Sergeant Fowler, he arrived eventually at destination, where both enjoyed the hospitality of the city force, who treated them to tea and canteen rock buns. Which many say are the best things in Birmingham. The buns, not the tea. This is terrible.

It was close to midday when they left, and they knew by

then about Albert. Communication between police forces is swift and sure. In the back of their unmarked car they carried three herberts of undistinguished aspect and surly mien. Youngish men who fitted nicely along the back seat. The detectives sat at the front, fully confident that these were not herberts who would launch sudden attack from behind. Certainly not with cuffs binding them together.

All went well until they had almost renegotiated that one-way system, guided by a sketch map supplied by a rubicund desk sergeant, when a fool of a learner driver came belting the wrong way off a roundabout and smashed right into the front of the car.

Broke Charlie Begley's pelvis. The seat-belt law saved him from worse, like diving through the windscreen. Saved Sergeant Fowler, too, traveling in the suicide seat. It shows how sensible is this law, even though being held back like that undoubtedly contributed to head injuries caused not only to him but to the herbert behind, who was flung forward by the impact, he and his mates all cuffed together, to whack with his forehead the sergeant's unfashionable coiffure, just above the short and curlies.

They took them all to hospital: Charlie and his pelvis, Sergeant Fowler and the herbert with crossed eyes and a tendency to babble; the two spare herberts with various scratches and contusions. From there, as soon as he was able, Detective Inspector Begley called the town station. The Birmingham police had done this already. They knew the situation, and it blew up on their territory.


Pete Parsons heard about it while he was sitting in the canteen with Wammo Wimbush, enjoying a solid lunch. A Detective

Constable Rumbold came by, bearing rissoles on a tray. He said, "Heard about Charlie Begley, gents?" and when they said they had not, he stayed to give them the picture. Not for long, because a canteen rissole must be eaten hot, if at all.

When he was gone, they demolished the apple crumble and cream with leaping spoons. Policemen, who at times of sudden action never know when they will eat again, do not leave food on the plate; and the summons would surely come. It did, before they were through the coffee. They tilted the cups, set them down, and went upstairs.

The Assistant Chief Constable said, "You've heard about Mr. Begley?"

"Yes, sir," said Inspector Parsons. "Bit of hard luck."

"Very. They're keeping him in hospital. Extremely awkward, at present. How are you doing with your Hollowbone case?"

"Hanging fire, sir. Can't push much further, unless we call it murder."

"I've been considering it. I'm afraid we still can't go that far. But I'm putting it out to the press as possible. Asking for the public to come forward if they think they know anything that might help—saw her going into the woods, out with men—you know the form."

"Fair enough, sir. May spur things along."

"I really haven't the manpower to mount three murder hunts—"

"Three?"

"The man stabbed this morning over at Bullingworth— he just died." Bullingworth is a town suburb. Nice area; few people get stabbed in it. "There's the Fish business. I can't cover another, without calling on the city force."

Calling for outside help is something no policeman likes to do. "Ah," said Pete, fully understanding. He knew a man had been found stabbed at Bullingworth last night, but he had not known the victim had died. That crowded the canvas, all right. Everything blows up at once.

"I am wondering, in view of the fact that you are already close to the Fish business"—it sounded as if the inspector's relatives were in trade—"if you shouldn't hand over the Hollowbone case. But I'm not sure whom to."

"I can handle both, sir," said Pete. "Nothing else on at the moment. And Sergeant Wimbush knew Fish well."

"Very well," said Sergeant Wimbush. "One of my best customers."

Not on. You, Sergeant, I shall be moving onto the Fish case." The ACC speaking. "You, Mr. Parsons, cannot be put onto two separate murders; strictly out of order."

"But one," said Parsons pointed out, "is not a murder."

"Exactly." The top dog suddenly grinned. "If it becomes one, obviously you will hand over, unless the Fish business is already cleared. Is it likely to tie you up for long?"

"I shouldn't think so, sir." Tell the top dog what he wants to hear; and what you want to believe, if you seek in on a case. "I imagine it will be pretty straightforward."

"Good. You'll be with Superintendent Churchyard."

"Right." Ted Churchyard. That was all right.

"Great pity about Mr. Begley. Makes an awkward hole. Still, so long as we can plug it."

"How's Sergeant Fowler, sir?" asked Wammo. It was time somebody mentioned the poor bugger. He was banged up too, you know.

"Mm? Oh—all right. Fine. Concussed, as I understand it. Thank you, gentlemen. That will be all."

On the way down the stairs, Wammo said, "Oh—by the way—I saw two of the girls last night. The lookers. In the Blue

90

Grotto. One of them—Helen—was with the Ross lad. She had a bloody great lovebite on her shoulder."

"How do you know it was a lovebite?"

"Oh, come on. She'd covered it with makeup. What else would it be?"

"Birthmark?"

"Ah. Hadn't thought of that. It looked like a lovebite."

"With your mind, it would."

"She'd got makeup all over it."

"How'd you know it was there, then?"

"She'd been dancing, got sweaty. It'd gone streaky."

"Couldn't see it naked and unashamed?"

"Well—no. Not all of it. But why cover it up, if it's a birthmark?"

"Be your age. And you with sisters. Very self-conscious at sixteen, aren't they? Spend hours in front of mirrors fretting over a pimple."

"Yeah. Maybe."

"The Ross lad was with 'em?"

"Yeah. Didn't mourn for long, did he? Probably out hunting for a replacement."

"By the sound of it, he'd found one. Bet he didn't stick any bite on her, wouldn't open his mouth far enough. Anything else turn up last night?"

"Not really, no. Plenty of kids knew her, nobody saw her. It's in the report."

"Uh-huh. Let's see if old Ted's in his office."

They turned left at the floor above ground level, which is where the three superintendents have their offices. It is written, the higher up the mountain, greener grows the grass. Up here was peace, and quiet in which a man might tend the leaping sheep of thought. Deep thought, as goes without saying.

Superintendent Churchyard was not in. They turned

away, traveling in silence to halfway down into the reception hall, when Wammo said,

"Just because they're all bug-eyed and dewy doesn't mean they're virgins, you know. Look what the doc said about their little mate."

"It's all in here, lad, have no fear." The inspector tapped his forehead. "It's all in here."

There is a book, and it must be signed by every officer leaving the station, stating below his often indecipherable scrawl time of departure and where he will be. If he moves on from there, he is supposed to radio or phone with verbal amendment, but he seldom does. Detective Superintendent Churchyard's scrawl said he was gone to the scene of Albert's murder. Half an hour ago he left, so he'd known he was booked onto the job for some time.

Well, he would, of course. And he would know his minions had been there already, that there was no point in his taking them down with him. He would know equally well that he would find there was nothing that they had not noted and would report to him; but the chief investigating officer obviously must see the place for himself.

Pete spoke to him from the communications room, via the radio set in his car. Mr. Churchyard said, "Ah—Pete. Good. Was there anything here I ought to know about?" He then listened while Mr. Parsons spoke for a little while, and when the matter of Albert's movements came up, from when the poor man left the station, he said, "Yes—I've seen the reports. Visits to Alderman Withers and Roger Dunbutt. Is that odd?"

"No. I don't think so. Went to complain, probably about harassment. Dunbutt got him the school job. Apparently Withers put a word in, he does a bit of do-gooding here and there."

"How's your other thing standing? Your girl caper?"

"Stock-still. Nothing stirring. The Old Man's letting the media in, asking for information."

"Yes, he told me. So you're spare?"

"Yup."

"All right. Suggest you go and have a word with Withers. And Dunbutt. Get it out of the way. I'll be back in five minutes; they're running these school herberts in from Brum. I'll handle that. Everything set up?"

"I'll check before I leave." But it would be. Uniform branch—backup teams—they all know what has to be done when a murder investigation must be mounted. House-to-house reports to be collated, files to be started, duties to be allocated—the details are endless. No officer or team of officers working solely in the field could possibly handle it alone, nor would he or they be permitted to try.

"Good. See you later."

# ·9·

There is some very fine real estate in and around the town, and
none fairer than the big houses standing well separated along
some of the wide, leafy avenues of Bullingworth. Nothing historic, no black-and-white Tudor or listed Queen Anne, all that
stuff was cleared away soon after the Second World War. In its
place they erected this solid-brick mix of superior bungalows
and six-bedroom demi-semi-mansions, all keeping themselves
to themselves in landscaped private grounds backed by the
woods. The people who live in these houses see very little of
each other. Except that they belong mostly to the same clubs,
the only time they nod to each other is in passing, walking the
pedigree or from limousines.

Detective Chief Inspector Parsons and Detective Sergeant Wimbush stood in a lovely room in one of the most imposing of these properties. They had been ushered in by a
maid, no less—how few of us own one, nowadays—to where
Alderman Withers stood with his back to the handsome marble
fireplace, his wife in one of the tapestry armchairs flanking it.
Inspector Parsons said,

"I'm sorry to bother you, sir. We called at the town hall;
they said you were gone home for lunch. Hope we haven't arrived in the middle of it."

"Not at all, Mr.—er—Parsons; not at all, we've finished." A big, solid man, this alderman, but grown soft from

good living and easy politics. He handled his beam with the skill of long practice. "How are you, Sergeant?"

"Very well, sir, thank you," said Sergeant Wimbush.

"Good. Good. And what can we do for you?"

"We've called about a man called Fish, sir," Parsons said. "I believe you knew him."

"Fish? Oh—*Fish*. Oh yes. Yes—Fish. Yes, indeed. Yes, we know him. Why?"

"According to our information, he visited you yesterday. At the town hall."

"That's right, yes, He had a problem."

"May I ask what problem?"

"Certainly you may. But I'm not sure that I should answer, officially. The matter is, in a sense, sub judice. Well, maybe not quite that, no action has been taken as yet. I can tell you for your private ear that it concerns you people."

"In what way?" As if I didn't know.

"This—er—robbery. At the Queen Victoria School. He is claiming harassment; apparently he was forced to submit to what amounts to accusation. Coerced into a police car, taken to the station. Browbeaten."

"Not coerced, sir. I believe he went quite willingly. And no accusation was made; he was free to go when he'd answered a few necessary questions."

"Were you concerned in the affair?"

"No. No, I just happened to be at the school about another matter."

"Your testimony would not really stand up, then, would it?" The heavy-featured, not too jowly face transmitted the beam warmly. Blandness is the salient skill in politicians. Often, the only one. It is never more avuncular than when they heft the hatchet.

It does not do for a policeman to debate so delicate a

matter with a local bigwig having great clout, especially when the bigwig's equally weighty wife sits in an impressive easy chair, listening to every word. The inspector sidestepped nimbly.

"Why did he come to you, sir?"

"I got him the job. Well—Roger Dunbutt suggested it. I put in a word with the education committee. We do a good deal of—er—charitable work. Don't we, dear?"

"Yes," said the wife. What lovely teeth they both had. You don't get those in discount stores. The alderman could well have afforded a hair transplant, to warm his balding pate. But perhaps a bald alderman has more prestige in council than a hairy one. He might have twisted his head this way and that in front of mirrors, trying various wigs before deciding against hair. Who knows what people get up to in the privacy of their own luxurious home, fitted throughout with rich-piled carpet and the very choicest in furniture?

"Prisoners' After-Care is one of our interests," he was saying. "We have been able to help several people. Jobs, supplementary benefits, accommodation. Personal problems, marital difficulties."

"Adjustment syndrome," said Mrs. Alderman Withers. Not Alderman Mrs. Withers, which is quite a different thing.

"Clothing. That sort of thing. When Roger feels he has a suitable case, he brings it to us if he thinks we can help."

"Uh-huh. I see. Do you have any idea what he planned to do with the rest of yesterday? I mean—did he mention going to see anybody else, anything like that?"

"My dear Mr.—er—"

"Parsons."

"Parsons. We hardly *knew* the man. I mean—why would he tell us? We don't mix in the same—the same—"

"Ambience," the lady said.

"Exactly. Thank you, dear. He'd been to see Roger—"

"Why all these questions, Mr. Parsons?" Mrs. Withers asked. "Have you arrested the poor man?"

"He's been killed, I'm afraid, madam. Murdered."

"Murdered?" This, at least, penetrated the alderman's bland front. He looked thoroughly shocked. "Good God!"

"Oh dear!" Mrs. Withers, too, appeared shaken by the abruptly broken news. "He—oh, poor man—who would—? He wasn't the one found stabbed in Filtmore Lane, was he?"

"No. That is quite a separate incident."

"Two murders?"

"That's right."

Mrs. Withers' hand had risen to the broad bulge of her handsome tweeds. Rings sparkled. "What is the world coming to?" she asked. Nobody attempted to tell her.

"Good God," the alderman said again. "Poor Fish. When did—?"

"Sometime between yesterday evening and this morning, sir. Somebody used a blunt instrument."

"But—who would—"

"That's what we are trying to find out."

"Yes. Yes, of course. Well—I don't see how we can help you."

"I doubt if you can, sir. We have to have a word with everybody who saw him recently—yesterday, in particular. He may have told somebody something to give us a lead. Names—somebody he was meeting—"

"He didn't tell me anything. Only about the harassment. The—interview, that is."

"Yes. Well—we won't take up any more of your time. If you do happen to think of anything, I am sure you will let us know."

"Of course," said the alderman; and his wife: "Of course

we will." She pressed a little button set into the arm of the chair. Somewhere in the house, no doubt, wherever the maid was, something electronic happened. The day of the tasseled bellpull is gone with the antimacassar. Grieve not for the manufacturers; they diversified into dressing-gown cords.

"Good day, then, sir—madam," the inspector said. "Thank you for your cooperation."

"Good day, Inspector, good day," they said; and the maid showed the policemen out. She appeared inside the door almost before they turned to it; and before they reached the car parked in the impeccable driveway, Alderman Withers was mopping his brow as he made for the whiskey, his wife watching him with contempt. Pete Parsons said as they drove away,

"He seemed to remember you, all right."

"Used to live on my beat over in Sickleworth, before they moved here. Done all right for themselves, haven't they? He was a common or garden councillor, in those days."

"Some are born great, some have greatness thrust upon them. The fault, dear Bombhead, is not in our stars."

"Nobody thrust anything upon him. Unless it was his wife. Power behind the throne, that one."


Mr. Dunbutt's neatly color-washed room stood close by the town hall, above the offices of a building society that owned the entire glass-and-concrete structure. Mortgage repayments must have been astronomical. He had two of these rooms: an outer one where a girl with red hair and eager eyes typed, filed letters and fingernails, answered and filtered telephone calls, and made coffee; and an inner sanctum where, apart from a cup taken at her desk, the coffee was drunk by old lags, young offenders, the wives and distressed relatives, the pregnant birds of young offenders, the boys back from Borstal, and all the seedy little people who live lives of amazing and futile complexity out of the respectable mainstream of this or any other town; and by Mr. Dunbutt himself, who sipped and nodded gravely at his desk, passing from time to time a packet of oatmeal biscuits kept in a drawer. Many of these little inadequates live upon crisps and mushy peas. They relish an oatmeal biscuit. Sometimes he sent the red-haired girl out for eclairs, very popular with the pregnant birdies.

His desk was in limed oak, to go with the relaxed atmosphere fostered by the general decor: light walls, bright curtains, two small modern demi-armchairs and a couch to match. Even the filing cabinet shone with unscagged buff paint. Since most of his clients dwelt among sagging furniture and a perpetual clutter or were fresh out of the nick, it is probable that the ambience kept them upright on the edge of the chairs; but to relax them in a sympathetic atmosphere was the idea. He was sitting at his desk when the detectives came in, the senior saying jovially,

"Hi, Roger. Thought you might be at lunch."

"I lunch early." Mr. Dunbutt's reply had a touch of stiffness in it. He hasn't forgiven, Pete thought, old Wammo's gag last time we saw him. He made sure his grin was working nicely. "It's a wise child that knows its own stomach," he said. "Spare us a minute?"

"I've people almost due."

"Won't take long, just a statutory part of the official channel." You can always nail people who work in social services by presenting words like "statutory," especially when you add "channel" and "official." "You heard about poor old Albert?"

"I have several Alberts."

He would have. It is an undeniable fact that the court

lists are peppered with older-generation Alberts. Behind them, among the round-about-thirties, come the Garys. The young are called Mike, or Sean, or Craig. "Albert Fish," the inspector said; and his sergeant added, "Got himself done, last night."

"Done? Beaten up?"

"Dead. Blunt instrument."

"Good God!" said Mr. Dunbutt, evincing shock. His plump white hands came from resting clasped upon the desk to gripping the edge of it.

"And it seems that you and Alderman Withers were the last to see him alive," the inspector said.

"I can't believe it. Does he know?"

He meant does the alderman know. Obviously, Albert knew. "We've just come from telling him."

"Good God."

And so to work again, the same old questions. Did Albert say where he was going, when he left here? To see the alderman. Yes, we know, we mean after that. No. Do you know who he associated with? No. But nobody criminal, he'd given all that up.

Do you know of any reason why somebody should thump him with a blunt instrument? No. Did he, Mr. Dunbutt, see him, Albert, often? Not recently, no. When he first came out he called often, but since he, Mr. Dunbutt, by the good offices of Alderman Withers, got him, Albert, the job— well, he wasn't on probation or anything, he didn't have to report. Always a good sign; it meant they were settled when they stopped coming in.

"A thankless task, you might say," the inspector said, "plucking all these little brands from the burning."

"We do not do it for thanks," Mr. Dunbutt told him. "We do it to provide support where it is needed." The stiffness, the use of the plural gave to the speech a regal tone.

"Well—thanks, Roger, we'll get out of your way." The two big men turned to the door.

Social workers who operate much among ex-cons prone to backsliding inevitably get to know something of police methods. "Did you put a tail on him when he left the station?" Mr. Dunbutt asked, knowing the answer. How else would they have known to whom Albert went?

"I didn't, not personally," said the inspector, "but yes, he had a tail."

"I should have thought they were the ones to tell you where he went."

"You have a point there, Roj, a very good point. See you, mate."

Again the two detectives walked down a flight of stairs. Again the man left behind mopped at his brow as he reached for the phone. Again the policemen exchanged their little private thoughts as they went. The junior said,

"Did he seem a bit on edge, to you?"

"Well," said his senior, "he would be. We hit him with it."

"No, I mean right from the start."

"You can only blame yourself for that. He hadn't gotten over your pudden crack."

"True," said Wammo Wimbush. "Very true. No sense of humor."

# ·10·

Detective Superintendent Churchyard had returned from the death site by the time they got back to the station. Had been back for some time, waiting for house-to-house team reports, double-checking to see that all was set to operate smoothly, speaking with the press, reading through primary forensic reports: plenty to do while he awaited the return of his acolytes and the delivery of the herberts from Birmingham; both of which events happened within minutes of each other.

They found him in his office, a man with a little hair left, tall even by police standards, and rail-thin. Never put an ounce on no matter how he ate. He looked at them across a cluttered desk and said,

"Ah—Pete. How'd you get on?"

"Nothing useful. Saw them both. He only went to squeak about Charlie."

"That was obvious. Press was on—local rags; I gave 'em the guff. They're running your appeal about the girl."

"Anything from the house-to-house?"

"Nothing so far. Nobody in the flats saw anything out of kink. People next door didn't even hear anything, nobody seen to call, no sounds of struggle. Didn't even see Albert. Well, they're all telly-bound, nowadays. There are two back doors into the block. Did we have 'em covered?"

"No. Only the front."

"Hmm. That's a bit of a cock-up, should have had somebody round there."

Small gray mark, sloped toward Inspector Begley. Pete said, "Charlie didn't know he was going to be done. It was only a light tail, just to keep an eye on him." The manpower situation, the cost of overtime both mitigate against prodigal use of a whole squad all round the clock, just to tab a minor robbery.

"Mm. The forensic reports don't tell us much—" The superintendent was reaching for the buff forms when his intercom buzzed. His big hand diverted, to flick the switch. "Yes? Good. I'll be right down." The switch clicked again. He began to elongate, upward out of his chair. "The herberts have arrived. Let's go and have a look at 'em."

They were quite ordinary herberts, of the type that embraces petty crime and periodical porridge as a way of life. By the records that came with them—the Birmingham police had done a rapid rundown—rather more ambitious and able than most, in that they specialized in school jobs, which, although they offer easy pickings, demand a degree of forward planning and orderly execution. They had been nabbed here and there—it was all in the records—but not every time, that's for sure. No violence used, ever, even when a caretaker appeared in Stroud to catch them in the act. They hailed from the Birmingham area, traveling to quite far-flung territories and back in stolen vans.

Only two were delivered, the third was still blinking from under bandages in a hospital bed. He was not missed—see one, you've seen 'em all. By the time the policemen came to the dungeon door—where the only sounds when a drunk is not singing and nobody is smashing up his cell are an occasional subdued cough, a nighttime snoring and farting, and the jangle of heavy keys—they had been locked into separate cells.

They were shocked. Shocked, not at the insinuation that they'd worked the trick in collusion with Albert—which they denied—but that they could be thought of as having done him in. Shocked at being faced suddenly with a detective superintendent, a chief inspector, and a detective sergeant, all in one pack.

Don't even know him, they said. Interviewed separately, of course, so that they could not stiffen each other. Who is he? Never fucking heard of him, you're fucking fitting us up. Begging your pardon, Guv. Honest—on my baby's life—I never fucking heard of him. Alarm showed in all the crafty eyes, of which each man had two. You're fucking fitting us up, they said.

"What do you think?" asked Superintendent Churchyard, when the second door had been slammed behind them and locked with that lonely jangle of keys.

"They're telling it straight," Pete said. He knew the superintendent asked the question only as professional courtesy. "Poor old Albert was clean, he wasn't mixed up in it."

"That's what I think," the tall man said, clacking along the stone corridor like a stork in metal diver's boots. Nobody asked the sergeant what he thought. It's the rich that get the pleasure. "What was he mixed up in, then?"

"Nothing, probably. He hasn't come on the books for a fair old time."

"But somebody knocked him off."

"Accident, maybe. Pissed—got in a fight."

"Which means he went out. In drinking time, unless he got pissed at home. So our lad didn't see him—so he went by the back door. Why? Because he'd spotted the tail, he was dodging. So why?"

Kite-flying, of course; but based on good, experienced thinking. Nothing startlingly original about it; police work has no real use for the smitten brow and the cry of eureka. Centuries of historic experience, plus his own long grafting, shape every policeman's thinking; and often they play like this: One advancing traditional theorizing, one acting stopper. So Pete said,

"Was he out in drinking time? Nobody saw him go out at all."

"Nobody saw him come in at all," said Wammo Wimbush.

"Suggest we give old George a blow, get a verbal on the PM."

Translation: The superintendent was announcing his intention not of walloping George, the little fat doctor, but of ringing him to obtain a verbal report. Not on the Prime Minister, but on the postmortem.

They went up again to the quiet and well-carpeted office—carpet ends at the doors of these rooms—and Mr. Churchyard made his call. The fat little doctor had Albert all gutted up on the slab with his skull open and his scalp rolled neatly back over his ears. His brains were in a dish. A gruesome trade, the pathologists', but they seem to enjoy it.

Before he put the phone down, the superintendent said, "All right, George, thank you. Yes, I'm coming over. About ten minutes." He then hung up, and said to the two men standing by, who had garnered only the uh-huhs and mms that had comprised his end of the conversation: "He wasn't pissed. About a couple of pints, that's all. And he ate a meal, not long before he died. Fish and chips. Do we have anything on the surveillance report? Did he stop anywhere to eat?"

"Nothing mentioned," said Pete.

"Pity. We'll have to call on 'em. Every fish-and-chips shop between—where?"

"Withers' place and his home?" Wammo suggested. "And the cafés—they do fish. Cod and chips, haddock and chips."

"It'd be well after he left Withers. Say, from eight o'clock on. Do we have a photo to flash?"

"Not at present." Pete Parsons. "Mrs. Fish may be able to supply one, when she gets here."

"Mm. Right. See to it, Pete, will you? I'm just going to take a squint at Albert." An unhappy chore, with poor Albert in his present state, but necessary. The senior investigating officer must see the body. "You'd better stay here, get a squad organized. Fish-and-chip shops, cafés and pubs. And look up all the restaurants with a license." This in case Albert ate and drank in a restaurant. Which was not likely; licensed restaurants cater more for the middle classes, they have ways of making the working man feel grubby; which Albert was. Strictly the fish-shop and sauce-bottle-topped-table type. But you cannot afford to ignore things.

"Right. Want me to buzz you if Mrs. Fish arrives?"

"I'll probably be back before that. If I'm not—yes, give me a yell." And Mr. Churchyard took one long stride away from the desk. It brought him to his hat, hanging on a peg behind the door.

They delivered Mrs. Fish during the afternoon. A tallish, rawboned, and rather grim-faced woman in a gray coat and a determined felt hat. She wore a pink nose and pink eyes, which may have been colored by weeping, although she did not look the sort of woman who cries easily. But then, those who cry hardest color soonest. It toned quite nicely, the pink with the gray.

Pete Parsons came with his mate to take delivery in the reception hall. He said, "Mrs. Fish—good afternoon. I'm sorry we had to bring you here under such melancholy—er—circumstances." Pompous condolence never did slide easily from his tongue; but a policeman is expected to approach close relatives of a murder victim with a touch of pomp. It sets the mental status quo, and this can be useful. Spread a little awe, in case you find later that they did it. Unease alone will often give them away, and most murder is domestic.

It does not mean that a bereaved person lacks feeling if the speech comes hard-edged and the eyes hold something of a challenge. Grief and shock show themselves in many different ways, and often the proudly reticent suffer more deeply than those who roar loudly, beating the breast. Mrs. Fish said, "I don't see why you did. I don't see why you couldn't take me straight home." Wasted no time on the sentimental just-widowed bit.

"We wanted a word with you first," said Pete. "And we'd rather like to see inside the flat, before anything is touched."

"Was he killed in the flat, then?" Obviously defensive, the abrupt tone. Keep your sticky hands off my private mind.

"We don't know yet, but we'd like to find out. We all liked Albert."

"Well—you knew him well enough."

"May we offer you something? A cup of tea?"

"I could use one."

"Sergeant Wimbush—see to that, will you? If you'll step this way, madam—Superintendent Churchyard will be joining us soon." The recall had been made, the superintendent was on his way in.

He took her to the upstairs office. It was more comfortable than his own, and the superintendent was not likely to object. He sat her in one of the small but comfortable chairs and took the other himself. He would have offered her a cigarette, but he did not smoke. The superintendent did, cigars only. There was a box in a desk drawer, he knew that; but you cannot offer a lady a cigar. Besides, while you may use a man's office, you must not interfere with his drawers.

"I haven't seen Albert for some years," he said. "Not since I was a beat copper. As a matter of fact, I hadn't even realized he was married."

"He wasn't," she said. "Not in them days, we got married a year ago. And I'd be obliged if you'd call him Mr. Fish."

"Ah—yes," he said. "Mr. Fish. Somehow, we always think of him around here as Albert. Ah—here comes Sergeant Wimbush."

"It's on the way," said Wammo, coming in. There was nowhere for him to sit except at the superintendent's desk, and that would have been a liberty, so he remained standing.

"Good," said Pete. "Fine." He turned his smile back to Mrs. Fish. "So—you've been married only a year. Would that have been before he started work at the school?" Was this lady's flat-of-the-hand what had kept Albert on the seeming straight?

"After. Soon after. I was working there. In the kitchen. School dinners."

"I hadn't realized Albert was married," said Wammo Wimbush. "Not now."

"Mr. Fish married Mrs. Fish a year ago," Pete told him.

"Ah. I knew he used to be; his wife's name was Liz."

"She deserted him, got a divorce." Mrs. Fish pursed her lips and nursed her handbag. "While he was in prison."

"Ah yes," Wammo said. "I remember." If he did, the

memory was very dim. Albert had not featured so large in his life that he worried over all his domestic problems. For the last three, four years, he had not featured at all. He vaguely remembered a mousy wife when Albert lived in an old terraced house on the slummy side of town. Rooting about in the memory would give her some kind of substance and form, but why bother? It was of no importance.

And now the tea had arrived, with biscuits. Three cups and saucers, one plate on a tray, borne by a burly constable with a short back-and-sides haircut tufted at the rear. Pete did the honors, suspending further official talk until he had sorted out such matters as what sugar she required, and how many biscuits. When they had stirred and sipped, he asked,

"Can you think of anybody who would have wanted to kill Alb—— Mr. Fish?"

She bristled in her chair with a hard and hostile eye. "Don't be ridiculous," she snapped.

Now Detective Superintendent Churchyard gangled in, angling his knees with the unthinking skill of long practice. He was, after all, a man of fifty, and he'd been angling them since he was a boy. Had to, or he whacked them on doorjambs. He smiled as he came, not too widely because under the circumstances it would have been unseemly. He said,

"Mrs. Fish—good afternoon. Thank you for coming."

"I was brought here," she said.

"Yes. I am Superintendent Churchyard. I see they're looking after you. Good. Good. I'm sorry we meet under such melancholy—yes. Don't want to rush you, but we're rather anxious to see the inside of your flat."

"Good job the tea's half cold, then. Don't you want me to identify him?" She snapped it, and drained the cup with little finger crooked.

"Yes. I'm afraid we do. Afterwards, we'd like to see that

flat first." Regulations, you see. Everybody knew it was Albert; but she'd have to identify, to make it official.

They traveled to the tall block in two cars: one policeman-driven, a spare constable as coroner's officer in front, the superintendent and Mrs. Fish in the back; the other, Pete's own, piloted by the owner, with his sergeant beside him. Mrs. Fish unlocked her front door. The investigating men followed her in.

She, if she dictated the furnishing, had a strong predilection for the modern-plastic school. Vinyl-covered three-piece suite, plastic flowers in a plastic vase on top of the plastic television set, Formica in the kitchen, nylon quilt in the bedroom, plastic lavatory seat with a fluffed plastic tie-over cover. If, as by the look and feel of it, she brought little comfort into Albert's life, nobody could doubt that she brought disciplined order. And rigorous cleanliness. Everything gleamed, amid a strong smell of plastic-squirter lavender and plastic air-freshener. The sergeant, who had known him best, looked upon it all with surprise as he readjusted his mental image of Albert's way of life. He was always such a scruffy little man, and he had lived in a scruffy little house.

There were no signs of struggle here, and no blunt instrument. Nothing. No disorder whatsoever. The lady did not enthuse when the superintendent asked that they be allowed to look through Albert's personal effects, but she raised no objection.

Nothing in Albert's best suit, his holiday clothing and jacket, hanging plastic-bagged in the wood-effect wardrobe. Nothing in his shirts and underwear, lying with socks reeking of cleanliness and impeccably folded in his drawer. Nylon shirts, spare working shirt, socks and everything, they had all been ironed. There was a small pink lavender block, holed like a doughnut, in with them, for striking terror into moths. They

110

came back into the living room where the window, hung with nylon curtains stirring in the breeze, looked into the dustbin alley. Mr. Churchyard said,

"Well now, Mrs. Fish—if you feel up to it, there are just a few questions I have to ask. Regarding Albert."

"I feel up to it," she said. "And the name is Mr. Fish."

The routine questions asked yet again, with no flashing illumination sparked from the answers. Some of the work had been done already, by gentle pumping in the car on the way over. It was not long before the superintendent was fingering his hat as he said, "Well—thank you very much, Mrs. Fish; you've been very helpful." She hadn't, she'd been brusque, monosyllabic, tight-faced. But to say so, that would never do. He indicated the window. "Do you always keep your window open?"

She looked at him as if to say: We have a right one here. "When it's warm," she said. "He'd have opened it, I suppose, when he got home."

Which meant that if he did go out, he went before the evening took on September edge. Probably before the sun went down. By the back door. Unseen by the tail keeping obbo at the front. Well, he was a cunning old pro, Albert. He might well have had the car spotted by then.

By when? Well—by whenever he went out. If he went out.

"Yes, of course," said Superintendent Churchyard. "Well—if you are ready, perhaps you will go with the—er—coroner's officer to—er—" And let's hope Fat George has tidied poor old Albert up a little. Rolled his scalp back up, at least.

She came out with them, and the very door seemed to snap behind them. The superintendent handed her over to the coroner's officer, and she was borne away. He'd have gone with her himself, but she was not likely to collapse; and there was work to be done, talking to be done, thoughts to be compared with his men here. No point in separating and waiting until he got back from the morgue and they all met up at the station.

Wammo spoke even before they got to Pete's car. "Bloody hell. What a Brahma. Bet she kept old Albert shuffling."

"Maybe she kept him out of the nick," Pete said.

"Maybe he'd sooner have been in it. Can't you see her and old Albert whacking away in bed?"

The late Albert's connubial cavorting held no interest, it seemed, for Superintendent Churchyard. He said, "More to the point—he wasn't clobbered in there, that's for sure."

"Unless," said Pete, "he was standing at the window, maybe opening it. Friend in for a beer, cup of tea. Stepped up behind him—wallop, and he falls out of the window. Exit friend, with blunt instrument. Probably a bit shaken, because he didn't expect him to fall out."

"Could be. My bet is, he was killed somewhere else and brought home."

"After midnight?"

"Probably. When our lad was gone."

"Bit chancy, lugging bodies about."

"It's been done. Hold him upright, pretend he's drunk."

"It could have been done before midnight," Wammo put in. "They could have come in from the other end of the alley; the lad wouldn't have seen 'em."

Still casting about. By now the car was under way, nearing the end of Albert's street. Pete changed down, to negotiate the corner onto the road that would take them back to the station. "House-to-house reports should all be in by now," he said. "Maybe somebody saw 'em."

But nobody had. The reports lay on Superintendent

Churchyard's desk when they regained his office, brought in and handed on for quick typing by those teams who had finished their allotted stint. Well, there were a few yet to come, perhaps they would yield. And the fish shops and cafés could be visited now, as soon as the darkroom opened to disgorge prints of Albert's dim features. No photos of him at home; but the old record one would do.

# ·11·

Young Helen had a bit of very bad luck that night. She was raped. Sergeant Wimbush, gathering overtime again—very legitimate overtime—saw her when he came back to the station after his evening spent among the fish-and-chip shops and terminating in the Rose and Crown, that pleasant little pub where Albert used to drink.

The upper brass was long gone home; not in any couldn't-care-less spirit, but because, as all the force knows, detectives who must carry the full weight of a murder inquiry do well to take advantage of the hiatus that comes so often at the beginning. The human blood and bone need rest, the brain dulls with exhaustion; and once things open up, these men may be out of bed, on their feet, sustained by quick snacks and cups of tea served wherever they happen to be, for days and nights on end.

Even in this waiting time they are not totally unencumbered. The brain is engaged, the body must be kept within reach of the telephone. When the call comes, there must be no hanging about.

So Pete Parsons was at home with his toothsome and resigned wife, who had hoped they might go to the indoor bowling alley but was settling instead to another evening with telly and video; and Ted Churchyard, whose wife had taken to knitting long ago, was fiddling with geranium cuttings in his

114

greenhouse when Wammo Wimbush, nothing positive gleaned from the fish run, came into the bar of the Rose and Crown and ordered himself a pint. Policeman's perk, the occasional pint charged to expenses. And it's fair enough: Free to choose, he might well be in a pub; but it would not be the pub he is in, shaping up to ask questions.

The landlord knew him. This is where he walked his beat, not long ago as veteran landlords see things—as through a glass, darkly. In the properly hoarse voice of the man who has long lubricated the speaking parts with whiskey, this matured-in-the-cask man said as he set down the pint:

"Don't see much of you these days, Mr. Wimbush."

"Don't get around here much, Mr. Bailey; nothing much seems to happen down this way. Cheers." Down went the first, long pull of beer. Delicious, after a slog around the fish shops.

"Here about poor old Albert, are you? Read about it in the papers."

The whole town would have read about it. Albert was all over the front page of the *Evening Courier*, circulation 85,000, and a free holiday in Majorca to be won. For two. First time Albert ever made the front page; in the old days he merited only an inside mention. Pity he wasn't here to enjoy it.

"That's right. Who'd have wanted to knock him off, any idea?"

"Nobody, I shouldn't have thought, poor old bugger. Bashed his head in, eh? Makes you think, dunnit?" He did not say of what.

"When was he in last?"

"Oo—don't really remember."

"He wasn't in last night?"

"No. He didn't come in every night; he got married again, you know."

"Yeah, I met her."

"We supplied the sausage rolls. Tell you who can tell you more about him than I can. Ernie Batling,"

"Ernie? Ernie Batling? Is he still about?"

"He's in the other bar. I'll call him in, if you want a word with him."

"No—don't bother, I'll go through."

With his pint in his hand, the sergeant went through the small door and into the scruffier of the two bars. Public, they called that side. Saloon they called this, and nobody had done much about tarting either. Which would explain why the pub held on to its regulars, those dart-and-domino, beer-wise men who scatter in despair and a welter of blasphemy before the encroachment of jukebox and plastic beams and chromium-plated lager fizzed up by plastic hoses or dropped pallid from the plastic bottle. The landlord, having to move only a few yards behind his bar to cover the distance, was there first. "Ernie," he said richly, "somebody wants a word." Isn't it funny, the things people say? You'd have thought this small and wizened Ernie in a bowler hat was a crossword-puzzle specialist, or a dab hand at Scrabble.

"Evening, Ernie," said Sergeant Wimbush in friendly fashion as he came through the door.

"Evening, Mr. Wimbush," said Ernie, not at all surprised to see him. Very much like Albert, he was, but a lot older. Partner with Albert on many a shop and housebreak in the old days, some said his mentor; and his bowler hat was greenish, inherited from his father's side—it was all the poor old bastard left—and older than he was. Better condition, too. "About Albert, is it?"

"That's right." The sergeant glanced around the booze-steeped bar. Nobody here but old Ernie, seated on the settle beside the open fireplace with his beer on the old oak table, and two nondescript laborer types morosely leaned against the bar itself, far end of the room. They looked at him with eyes that had gazed down newly dug holes at many a water main. He said to the landlord as he lowered himself onto the seat beside the old man, who smelled of elderly sweat and prison lockers: "I'll have another of the same. And one for Ernie."

"Ta, Mr. Wimbush," said Ernie. He had come to the age when the pipes begin to quaver. "Doan mind if I do."

"Well now," the sergeant said, "what do you know?"

"Nuffin, Mr. Wimbush. I doan know nuffin no more. Nobody tells me nuffin about nuffin no more, since I retired."

"You didn't retire, Ernie, we retired you. One more, you'd have copped PD."

"Doan be like that, Mr. Wimbush. We turned it in, me and Albert both. Doan pay, do it? Well, it's all right when you're young and sprightly and that, but not when your legs is going. I never bin better orf nor what I am today."

"What are you doing now, then?"

"National Assistance, ain't I? Then there's me old age pension. Pay the rent and all, they do. Wish they'd had it when I was young. I'd never've took to thieving."

"What about Albert? Who'd want to knock him off?"

"I doan know, Mr. Wimbush, straight up. What'd they go and do Albert for, he never done no one no harm. We never got mixed up in nuffin like that. No violence."

"Who was he mixing with, do you know?"

"Nobody. Not since he started work up at that school."

"Look, Ernie," said Wammo Wimbush. "Albert was a friend of yours. Right?"

Suddenly, the old man's rheumy eyes were filled with tears. "Like a son, he was," he said. The beer arrived. He picked up the glass, said cheers, and resettled himself with a swig.

"Cheers," said Wammo. "So—I want the bastard who did him. You want the bastard who did him. Right?"

"Well—yeah."

"Come on, then. Anything. Anything at all."

"Mugged? There's a lot of it about."

"He wouldn't have been where we found him."

The old man hesitated, took another swig at his beer. "Did he have a roll on him?"

"Roll?"

"He had—well, a roll. Tell you the truth, I'd bin wondering if he'd bin doing a bit. You know—the old caper. Or something."

"Why?"

"Well—he was a bit flush lately. You know—drinking shorts. I had a few orf him, he just used to order 'em in, say get that down you. Give me a tenner, lars Christmas."

"Well, he was working, wasn't he? And what about his wife—was she earning? She's a cook—"

"Not her. Chucked it in when she married him. He should never have done it. No. There was—look—he went racing a lot. Took me, once. Lost on every bleeding race, lot of money. Paid it orf a roll, fivers. I told him he ought to go easy, he said plenty more where that comes from."

"Uh-huh. He didn't say where he was getting it?"

"Come orf it, Guv."

"You didn't ask?"

"You doan ask fings like that." The old man looked quite shocked. "Not my bleedin business, was it?"

Well, this was something. A little something, but something. Only small money was found on Albert. He *could* have been mugged—leaving the flat, passing the alley, dragged into it.

But no—not before midnight, not at the front end. And

if near the back entrances, at the other end—what mugger would carry him all the way along the alley to dump him this side of the bins? They'd open the alley gate, bundle him in, and leave him there.

"Ernie," said Sergeant Wimbush, "give it thought. You know the sort of things I want to know. Anything comes to you, give me a bell. Same old number."

"Yeah, Guv. Yeah, I will. Like a son, Albert was."

"Happy Christmas."

"Happy Christmas."

They must have been among the first this year in all Christendom to exchange the seasonal greeting.

On his way out of the pub, the policeman checked with the landlord. Yes, Albert had taken to shorts, with a chaser. Well, he was working, wasn't he? You don't ask everybody who buys a tot where he got the money. No, he never flashed a roll, not in here. And he didn't drink much, maybe four or five on a Saturday, that was about his limit. No, he didn't hang about with anybody else, only old Ernie. No, he never come in with the wife. Look, Mr. Wimbush, I wouldn't tolerate nothing bent, you know that. I can smell 'em, any of 'em starts getting into a regular huddle here, I blows 'em out. You know me.

The sergeant did not go directly back to the station. He diverted to his home, where he knew he could get a slice of decent stand pie with salad on the side, even if the plate upon which it arrived hit the table with a bang that made the tomato jump. They were fighting again. He left with belly furnished but lips unkissed, wondering if the stupid bastard who said it first really believed that marriages are made in heaven.

The stars were out by the time he got to the station, winking and blinking against their remarkable backcloth. He greeted a man here, exchanged a gag with a man there, got his hand slapped in very friendly fashion when he laid it briefly with exaggerated growling on the trim serge buttock of a rather pretty WPC. These pleasant things attended to, he went into the CID room, where he pooh-poohed the chances of Arsenal winning *any* league championship, let alone the European cup, before settling down to type the report upon his long day's activities. And when he came out, headed for home and a time in bed at last, he came upon young Helen Jonas.

# ·12·

It was Albert's death that brought Helen out tonight. She read about it in the local paper, soon after she came home from school. If the police had notified Miss Wellborn-Davit—and they might have done, to explain why her caretaker had suddenly vanished—the lady had wisely preferred not to spread the news. It came as a terrible shock, therefore, when Helen picked up the paper and found the front page covered with Albert.

She could not leave the house again directly, she had not yet had her tea and she'd already announced a quiet evening at home, the three of them having agreed that this was the thing to do while they worried and waited for Albert, or somebody, to get in touch. Nor could she use the telephone to ring the others. It was in the living room, and so for most of the time was her mother. At the other ends, Angie and Patricia were similarly placed, with additional big-eared and nosy complication. One had two young brothers, the other a smaller sister.

She picked at her tea, which caused her mother to ask if she was sick or something. She said, in the truculent and aggrieved manner adolescent girls favor for use about the house, couldn't she be not hungry without being sick or something? To which her mother replied, don't use that tone to me, my girl, you don't know when you're well off, there's plenty in the

Third World who wouldn't know a fish finger if you stuffed it up their nose.

After tea, and a nervous hour while she wondered what, if anything, to do, she said, "Think I'll go out."

"I thought you said you were staying in," her mother said. "I thought you were going to wash your hair."

"Changed my mind, haven't I?" she said. "I suppose I'm allowed to change my mind?"

"You needn't think," said her father, home by now and settling to the telly, "that you're too big to feel the back of my hand."

She never did feel the back of anybody's hand, and never had. All the violence in the house was verbal. She left with a slam of the door behind her and the sullen sulk of her face. It faded swiftly, as it does from any normal teenager when she is moving away from her home, replaced by the translucently demure doe-eyed look of the young girl tripping about a young girl's business.

The others had read the paper. Patricia had already arrived when she reached Angela's home, but it was some time before they could talk freely. They had to spend half an hour discussing the terrible news with Angela's mother and father— who also read the paper—and admiring a dress that her mother was constructing from a paper pattern and a vent of blue velvet picked up cheap in the market. Angie, having said she was staying in, had been immediately co-opted into pinning hems and tucking bits in, and cutting sleeves while her mother treadled away on an old but grimly serviceable sewing machine. "Last for donkey's years yet, that will," the father of the house said whenever his wife hinted for a new one.

It was after eight when they managed to take a walk in the nearby park, beyond observation and earshot of the mother, the father, and the one of the young brothers who had not gone out for the evening. As they walked, they talked. That stands to reason. It's what they came for, and at no time do young girls walk in silence. Not even in school crocodile.

Truth is, they were badly shaken, even frightened, because at bottom the girl is a catgut-strung creature, beset by hormonal changes and unsettling glandular developments that lumber her with violent emotional instability. They are extremely prone to panic, especially when more than one are gathered together and spreading it about a bit.

So they walked, and they talked: about Albert; who could have killed him and why. Whether it had anything to do with them; whether he had anything to do with the school robbery, he having extraneous interests that none of them knew about; frightening themselves with the thought of two deaths, one definitely by murder, coming so close to them, so close together.

They walked along the road through the park, passing the shelter near the boating lake where two lads were glue-sniffing. Dusk was down, and plump Patricia—the most panic-prone of all—physically shivering in the September chill as they came back by the paths that lead through the rose garden and along by the upper railings, Helen saying,

"We'll have to see Roger."

"No," said Patricia. "No—we mustn't see *anybody*—the police will be watching—"

"No, they won't. Why should they?"

"Albert was *murdered*—they'll watch *everybody*." People in panic invariably populate their world with omnipotent policemen. "Why did they come to see us again about Debbie?"

"Debbie fell in the river."

"Then why are they asking anybody who saw her to come forward?"

"Who are?"

"The police are. It's in the paper."

"Where?" By their further stiffening, neither of the other girls had seen it. They never got past Albert.

"Inside, near the telly programs."

A pause, while Helen and Angela flashed the matter through their minds. Helen spoke again, uneasily. "That doesn't mean anything, they have to do that."

"What was that one thing in the Blue Grotto, then?"

A further pause. Angie said, "I don't think we should do anything. I think we should just—lie low. Not go near Roger. Or Paul."

"That sergeant saw you go with Paul," said Patricia.

"I've got to go in," Angie said. Her mum had told her to be back in half an hour; and another truth about panicking young people: They suddenly begin to obey implicitly such parental commands, partly from acute need to be child again, and not responsible, partly to avoid awkward questions. "We can't do anything now; we'll have to get to school early, talk about it before we go in."

The others, too, knew that nothing could be done tonight, that the time had come for them to go home. They parted at the park gates, Angela turning before she Bambi-walked across the road to say: "They can't demand to see our post-office books, can they?"

"Who?" Helen demanded. "Who's going to demand anything?"

"Well—anybody." And away went Angela.

Patricia left, going in the opposite direction. Almost scurrying, as though she needed to be off the streets. Helen turned back to cross the park, shortcut to home.

The two lads saw her coming. Tucked into the shelter out of sight, they had seen her before as one of the trio walking together and had drooled and chortled the normal obscenities. Now she was alone.

They were not far gone into the glue-high. Not far enough to be blinded to anything other than hallucination. "Corr-rr," said one. "Thass her, thass the one I wanna fuck. Corr-rr—cooten 'arf do her a bitter good."

"Why doan we, den?" his mate said. "Nobody abaht, is dere?"

She ran. Any young girl should do likewise, when she finds two big herberts bursting from a shelter and pounding toward her in a park on a dark night. The male is built longer in the leg, narrower in the hip, and swifter. "Let me go, let me go, let me go, you bastards," she screamed when she was grabbed, at the bushy corner of the lake not far from the lower park gates. And she bit furiously at the hand that came over her mouth, even as she lay under the lad squatting on her breasts to pin her arms with his knees while his mate ripped off her skirt and tore the little pants away. "Corr-rr," he said, "look at dat! It's grinnin' at me. Move yer arse up, less 'ave a look at 'er tits."

He went first, while his mate held her. Then they swapped over. It was unlucky for them, and perhaps as unlucky for Helen, that a dedicated jogger should come prancing down the path going nicely with knees well up, and that this jogger should be an off-duty policeman called Gladwyn, PC Joe Gladwyn. Mind you, they asked for it, they were practically out in the open. That's what the glue can do.

The first goer, holding her now while his mate performed, saw the big man coming almost as the copper, rounding the bend, saw what was going on. He shot up and took to his heels. Perhaps he sounded warning; but the lad at work was fast approaching the point of no return, he was grunting and panting and couldn't have stopped now if he'd wanted to. Even as he groaned his ultimate groan the policeman arrived, to grab and pull him off and hold him dangling, caught between astonishment and pumping ecstasy. Very muscular man, PC Gladwyn.

Because it was nearby and he was all alone, not quite sure how he should proceed—Helen would obviously have to go to hospital for examination—PC Gladwyn got them through the park gates, where he flagged down a motorist who took them to the station. Helen wanted to go home; but the policeman said, "We can't let you do that, dear, can we? Not with this gentleman's rug wrapped round you." Because the lads, when they tore her skirt and pants off, flung them aside and they landed in the lake. PC Gladwyn retrieved them, he even lent her his jogging singlet to cover the parts that must not meet the eye; and now she was wrapped in a woolen plaid rug, courtesy of the motorist who kept it on the back seat, to save the upholstery from hairs of the dog.

And this is how it happened that Detective Sergeant Wimbush, headed at last for home, came upon a knot of men standing in the reception area and three females seated upon the bench there, one wrapped in a plaid rug.

He knew there had been a rape, the very air bears all incoming cases about a police station; but no names were given. Now he saw Helen, and his seasoned mind slotted it all together. She the victim, wrapped in the rug; beside her a WPC, and the older woman would be her mother; they would have rung her parents at once. The angry-looking man would be her father, one was Joe Gladwyn in his jogging gear. One was Sergeant Hogge, who would have taken the matter in hand. The other was the little fat doctor, who must have been raked out in a hurry.

Presumably, they were bringing an ambulance round.

Presumably, too, the parents left home so hurriedly they'd neglected to bring clothes. Perhaps they did not know she was wrapped in a rug, they probably slammed the phone down and set off running before anyone could tell them.

He did not stop to speak. It is no time to chat with a girl, just after she has been raped. She had not seen him, she was speaking sulkily to her mother. He veered, and went through the swing door that leads to the side stairs and the canteen. He could gather the details when they were gone, from the Incidents Book and from chatting around.

He bought himself a cup of tea, and drank it. When he came down again to the reception area, the people were gone, Joe Gladwyn, Sergeant Hogge, little fat doctor, and all. He gathered information from the big black book—bald outline only, but quite enough for an experienced man. And then he went home, where his wife greeted him frigidly and made some more tea.

When he judged that the doctor would be back from the hospital, he rang his number. The doctor said, "I trust you are not hoping for a cozy chat. I've had a dinner party ruined already, you know."

"Yes, I'm sorry, Doc," said the sergeant, who didn't know. "Won't keep you long. You examined this kid, this Helen Jonas girl."

"I didn't come out to buy turnips."

"Did she have a mark on her shoulder?"

"She had several marks. Bruises, scratches—"

"I was thinking more of a lovebite."

"There is a mark, yes. I shall be making a full report."

"Older? I mean—done before tonight?"

"Yes. If you're asking me whether she—indulged—the answer is yes. Frequently. She received the lad without trouble."

"Ah. No injury?"

"None. Not to the genital tissues." A pause. The doctor added, "She was wearing a cap. As a matter of fact, her general condition suggests that she is highly experienced."

"Ah. You reckon she was under age when she started?"

"Definitely. She's only a couple of months over sixteen, apparently."

"And she's been at it longer than that?"

"Unless she's been doing it night and day."

"Thanks, Doc," the sergeant said. "Much obliged to you."

He replaced the phone and went in to see what was for supper, at about the time when the second jolly little rapist came home after wandering about in combined trepidation and glue-haze, walking straight into the arms of two coppers waiting for him. It had not taken long to persuade his good old buddy that he should disgorge the name and address.


Detective Inspector Parsons awoke next morning in the way that brings comfort and sure knowledge, provided he loves the woman in his bed, that something of ineffable good is left to a man in this sin-crusty world. His wife, who had rolled over in the night to present buttocks and back, for neither of which he had anything but the most sincere admiration, had rolled back while they were asleep, and made the lovely gesture of trust and affection—the more telling because she did not know she had made it. His opening senses found her snuggled, for there is no other word: head in to his shoulder, leg across his, body abandoned unguarded, close in to him. He came back from wherever he had been wandering by night, and absorbed very peacefully the soft body warmth, the soft regular breathing, the scented softness of her hair.

It does not last, alas, this ineffable waking daze. A few seconds—a minute, given very fair weather—and in comes thought, and memory of yesterday, and remembrance of all the stress and fret to be faced today before the winning back to bed at night. And it comes rarely; more rarely, perhaps, to detectives than to your luckier men. Firstly, few detectives love and are loved sufficiently. Secondly: They go to sleep, they wake up with such nasty things on their minds.

Wonder about the time is often first indication that the party's over. By the time the inspector had turned his head to focus upon the small, smug clock squatting evilly on the bedside table, carefully because he did not want to wake the wife, Albert was here already; moving into the perfumed garden, bringing the stink of a new corrupted day.

He lay for a little orientating time, breathing in the warm, scented softness of her and her hair, enjoying the good strength of a morning erection before easing his body gently away and out of bed. He found his slippers, pulled on his dressing gown, and left the room quietly. No phone call in the night, so nothing had happened.

Five minutes later he was back, bearing a cup of tea and the biscuit barrel. He kissed her awake, saying, "You going to lie here all day?"

"What time is it?" she asked, almost before her eyes were in focus. You see? We are conditioned to it, governed by it.

"Quarter past eight," he said, and eased her left breast over her nightgown, to kiss it.

"Nice. That's nice." She wouldn't have meant the clock reading. "What time are you going in?"

"Soon as I've showered and you've made me a bit of breakfast. Drink up, there's a good girl." And he left her again, sitting up lovely in bed, one breast in and one breast out, rooting in the barrel for a chocolate biscuit.

We should all be so lucky. Not every pretty woman will sit like that, feeling good because he just confirmed again that her breasts are worth kissing in the morning. Not when all the tangible gifts he brings are a cup of tepid tea and what she hopes will be a chocolate biscuit, the last of which he may even have eaten himself before coming up, leaving only disappointment and a ginger nut.

They were in the kitchen when the telephone rang, he almost dressed to go, she in her dressing gown. He said: "I'll get it," and went out into the hall. Halfway through a cup of coffee when he came back, she asked the normal question.

"Who was it?"

"Station," he said. "They just had a call. Asked for me. When they said could they pass on a message, whoever it was said they saw a lad going into the woods with the Hollowbone girl the other evening. Red school blazer, gray piping, gray slacks. Then they rang off."

"Ah. Well—it'll give you something to think about."

"Mm. Gabbled it all. High voice—a kid. Or a girl."

"Hoax? Dare you to ring the cops?"

"Could be. But they asked for me, by name."

"Didn't the *Courier* ask people to get in touch with you?"

"Did it? I don't know." He hadn't done more than skim the evening paper. "Where is it?"

"I just wrapped the tea leaves in it, slung it down the disposal unit. Sit down and eat up your sausage before it goes off."

# ·13·

Other people had died in the night, and given birth, and performed with varying degrees of satisfaction the hot and humorous operation that gives rise to giving birth, and walked up and down with babies, and quarreled bitterly and thumped each other, and had babbled, lost in the starry and dangerous miracle, that nobody, ever, loved as they loved, and generally behaved as people in any town anywhere behave every mortal night. Few are so lucky as the Parsons, come through the treacherous frenzy of falling in love to the deeper, dependable love beyond. Among the myriad less lucky, less crooned over by this night were Wammo Wimbush and his disenchanted lady; Roger Dunbutt, who lay awake, very worried; and, of course, young Helen. However unvirgin a girl may be, rape is a terrible thing. Even where there is no physical injury, it brings bad dreams.

Roger arrived in his office, as Pete Parsons sat down to finish his sausage. Eight forty-five. Early, his starting time was nine o'clock; but he wanted to be there before the red-haired girl arrived. She listened in on phone calls, he knew she did; and he could not ring from home, because of his widowed mother.

He rang Alderman Withers, who identified himself in his underpants. Well-to-do businessmen do not have to gallop in anywhere at any particular time, and the alderman was just dressing, pink and marbled from the shower. He snapped, when he knew who was calling: "What the hell are you doing? I told you to stay off the phone."

"Have you heard anything?" said Roger. "Have they been on to you again?"

"Why would they be on again?"

"They won't just leave it, will they? They'll be probing into all his affairs. And they haven't finished with Debbie."

These things he had said, in essence, into the same ear three times before: once during the red-haired girl's lunch break, once during her afternoon tea break, and once when she was gone, before he left for home and his widowed mother.

Obviously, the happenings of yesterday had played progressively upon him, each successive call showing his reaching out more desperately for reassurance. This morning, after his sleepless night, you could hear the cold sweat as he started to speak. Alderman Withers had had enough, he carried worries of his own. Venomous in his underpants, the very belly quivering with it, he snarled: "Get off the line. Don't ring me again. Don't come near, do you hear me? Stay away. Stay away." And he slammed the phone down.

His formidable wife, in her padded dressing gown with her curlers still offering severe optical injury to anybody who might cuddle her—but then, who would?—said, "Dunbutt?"

"The fool," snarled Alderman Withers. "He's panicking. *He's* the danger—*he's* the danger." He was glaring, quivering, livid.

"Stop it!" she commanded. Even in her curlers she could command. "Get your clothes on. And calm down." The Dunbutt panic was unsettling him, she could see it. This they could not afford.

The tone of command stiffened him immediately. It always had, at times of crisis over thirty years. Pompous and basically weak men lean heavily, if often with secret resentment, upon the commanding women who marry them. Obediently, he stopped quivering and sat down to don his socks. "He's the danger," he said again; and added with a foot in the air, "He might even go rushing to the police."

She was seated now at her dressing table, and the curlers were clonking into the tray. "Not him," she said. "He's not such a fool as that."

"We don't know what kind of fool he is," he said, "when he's rushing about in a panic."

When Helen met her friends in the playground this morning, at about the same time—it was all happening, all happening—and told them, because they didn't know, that she was raped last night, they said what! and who by? Where?

"In the park," she said. "By the lake, after I left you. Two fellers—they came out of the shelter. I couldn't run fast enough."

"*Two* fellers?" said Angela. "Twice?"

"Twice," Helen said. "They'd still have been at it now, but this feller came along. Jogging. He turned out to be a policeman." And she told it all, the way it was.

Neither Angie nor Patricia asked if she sustained injury; and not because her presence here proved, surely, that she had not. Their minds were busy with other things. As a matter of fact, the girl's parents had wanted her to stay home, at least until the family doctor had looked her over; but she had reason enough to say she was all right, don't fuss, and to come to school anyway.

"Did they examine you?" Angie asked.

"Of course they did."

"Did they say anything about—?" Young girls do not need to be explicit, each knows that they all know much, much more about the physical effects of repeated intercourse than comes to them via biology lessons.

"Why should they? I'm sixteen, I don't have to be a virgin."

"Did they tell your mum and dad?"

"No." She knew they hadn't; there would have been a terrible fuss.

"Have you got to see the police again?"

"They didn't say so. No. They've got the two fellers."

Here, of course, she was quite wrong. The police do not take the chief protagonist in a rape case home and forget about her, just like that.

Patricia's voice was coming from her in something like a squeak this morning. She used it now. "What about—"

"Sshh," said Angie, as another girl approached with a view to chat. "Here comes Samantha Rugg. Pull yourself together, Fatty, you look a raw suet pudding."

The first thing Pete Parsons did when he arrived at the station was to look at the Incidents Book. Every detective does this as soon as he comes in through the CID door and has walked along the passage leading into the reception-desk area. It tells him at a glance whether anything has happened bearing upon his cases, or whether he knows something about something that may be of help to colleagues, or whether it is likely that he will be lumbered with addition to his workload.

The rape was noted: time of incident, time of Helen's arrival, everything. He recognized the name, his mind fitted the correct image to it; but nobody could give him full details.

The policemen concerned had all gone home. So he called in at the switchboard, who could tell him no more about his treble-voiced caller than they already had. He went up to look at Superintendent Ted Churchyard, already in his room and studying various sheets of official paper; and so on to his own office, there to study his own bumph and to await the coming in of Sergeant Wimbush, him and his verbal report upon his nosing around of last evening.

The sergeant arrived very soon. Pete Parsons said, "Morning, Wammo. You know that kid Helen Jonas? She was raped last night."

"I know," said Wammo. "I saw her."

Mr. Parsons looked disappointed. "Didn't do it, did you?"

"No, but I'll tell you what—I checked with the quack. That's not a birthmark, it's a bite. And she's been hard at it, like her little mate."

"Ah." The inspector did not commend his henchman for taking quick advantage of the situation to clarify a point in a roundabout way. A CID copper is expected to use his loaf. "Interesting."

A pause, while he chewed his lip. The sergeant said, "Do we want to know?"

"We might. We might." There would be criminal offenses about if these kids started doing it before they were sixteen. As obviously they did, in a very determined way. "Did you have a word with her?"

"No. I was just going home, it wasn't the time. Her parents were here—the quack—they were taking her for a hospital check."

"Did they injure her?"

"Only a few exterior bruises. The doc says she could

take a donkey." If he did not exactly phrase it like that, it's what he implied.

"Mm. What about Albert?"

"Saw old Ernie Batling, in the Rose and Crown."

"Old Ernie? Is he still about?"

"They only fade away. Says Albert's been flashing a roll around. Buying him shorts, took him to the races. Lost a bun-dle—said there was plenty more where that came from."

"Did he?" That, too, was interesting. No need to dig at it, Wammo knew as well as he how interesting it was. If there were more, the sergeant would have mentioned it, now and in his written report. The inspector began to rise from his desk. "Let's go and see Ted Churchyard," he said. On the way up the stairs he told Wammo about the morning call.

Ted Churchyard already had mulled over Wimbush's written report, and found it—well—interesting. He found the sergeant's verbal equally so. Nor did he show boredom when Pete Parsons said,

"Harking back to my other matter—we had a notice in the *Courier* last night. Somebody rang anonymously this morn-ing, said they saw the girl going into the wood with a lad, and I think I know the lad. And one of her friends was raped last night."

"This Helen Jonas," said the superintendent. State-ment, not question. Only one rape was in, and never a sparrow falls without a top-line policeman mentally filing the thud.

"Yes. I thought I might go and have a word there."

"Don't see why not." Never ask why. When you team with a man long known as solid and upward-bound, let him handle his work in his own way. Probing Albert for now could be only plod, plod, plod, undertaken by a team of men whose particular forte was plod. Waste of the more leaping brain. Let it go and keep itself happy and honed, until you really need it. "I'll handle the press conference."

Parsons spoke to Wimbush. "Who's got the rape?"

"Johnnie Hogge. But he won't be in." Policemen on nights must go briefly to court, if charges are to be preferred against clients gathered in under the moon. Then they roll into their beds.

"Uh-huh. Give him a bell. If Brenda answers, tell her not to wake him up, nothing urgent, we're just going to have a word with his case." Courtesy call only, this. When two coppers have interest in a case from different angles, both will need to interview; but professional ethics state clearly that the man with the secondary right should not barge in bullheaded without so much as a nod at the man with the direct interest. "Tell her to tell him it's to do with the Hollowbone caper. I'll see him about it later."


Miss Wellborn-Davit received them once again in her office. She croaked in that cow-frog voice: "Raped? Surely not! Helen Jonas? Poor child. Poor child. Why has she said nothing to me? Or to her form mistress? Really—what *has* become of us this week?" Well may she have wondered. First, Deborah's death; then robbery, and the caretaker removed by police car, the police all noncommittal; the caretaker found murdered; and now this.

Neither of the policemen attempted an answer. Surely she could not have expected one. And yet she sat there with her mouth left half open and her eyebrows raised. So Pete said, "It's certainly been happening, hasn't it?"

"We've had it before," said Miss Wellborn-Davit.

"There was Edna Biggs, 1976. But she led the boy on, of course. It's always a danger. Now she's got three of her own. Married him. Pity, I always thought she'd do well. I expect you want to see her."

Clearly, she did not mean the unfortunate Edna Biggs. "We came for a word with her, yes," the inspector said.

"I—er—does the law—I believe she should not be questioned without her parents being present."

She was perfectly right. But there are times when a policeman's investigation can be terribly hampered by the presence of fluttering parents, or angry ones, or even an argumentative solicitor. Pete had, in fact, played it by the book. He sought the girl first at home, believing she would not be at school this morning. Nobody at all was at the house, and a neighbor said both parents were at work. She even named the firms.

So he rang the mother rather than the father, knowing the opposite sexes tend more readily to take the attractive other on trust. He led her, be it admitted, to understand that he was merely following up on the rape, with no more than routine in hand. He did not want to start outrage and recrimination within the family; you can shut down the most promising lead that way, with a bang.

So now he was able to smile candidly upon the headmistress and say, "We've had a word with her parents. They have no objection to our seeing her alone."

Use of the plural is effective, as Royalty knows well. It directs the addressed beyond the little individual to the awesome aura surrounding a mystic and stern-eyed Power, brooding over all. Miss Wellborn-Davit hesitated for a moment only before she dismounted from behind the desk, saying,

"Will you wait here?"

Helen, when she was ushered in, showed no sign that

her heart was beating high. She looked exactly as a schoolgirl should: demure in her neat uniform, very clean and virginal, the spotless blouse hiding any mark on her shoulder. Inspector Parsons displayed the warm smile. "Good morning," he said. "Here we are again."

"Sit down, dear," said Miss Wellborn-Davit solicitously. Headmistresses do turn solicitous toward pupils who have been raped, or even those who report with a nasty cough. "No need to be upset."

Well, there was nowhere for the child to sit. Two guest-chairs only in this room, with a policeman on each. But Sergeant Wimbush got up. The girl sat down.

"Just a few questions we need to ask," Pete Parsons said.

"Why didn't you *tell* me, dear?" croaked the little black-haired lady. "You should have *told* me." She set herself firmly on her little legs and folded her arms. Clearly, she intended to stay, seeing herself as bound to be parent-by-proxy.

And rightly so, working by the book. But she had to go. Girls and policemen have their rights, too; and one must not be forced into the humiliation of having her secret life probed by the other in the increasingly scandalized presence of her head-mistress. And not only that: The clamming up that cannot be prized apart in such a presence will severely interfere with the policeman's right to extract answers that he might get by cut-ting a corner or two in private; and this is denying him the right to practice his craft unhindered. Pete Parsons kept the smile going, but his voice was very firm as he said,

"Miss Wellborn-Davit, I must ask you to leave us alone."

The lady's eyebrows shot toward the hair. "Alone?" she said. The late Dame Edith Evans bestowed a somewhat similar delivery upon a handbag.

"Alone, madam, if you don't mind."

Sergeant Wimbush, who knew the game well, was already at the door and opening it. She glanced from one to the other. They beamed upon her blandly. "Well—" she said. "Well—I'm not sure—well!" And she marched from the room. The sergeant closed the door.

"Well now, Helen," the inspector said, "that was a nasty experience you went through last night. No grave ill effects, I trust?"

Her reply was very soft. The demure maiden's shy whisper. She was playing it for all it was worth, this morning. "No. Thank you."

"No. The doctor said no physical injury resulted. And the psychological shock would not be so great as if you'd been a virgin. Would it?"

"I—er—I—er," she said; and stopped.

He waited for a moment. She remained silent, her eyes gone big and warily guarded. He said, "He says you are a long way from that. How long since you began?"

"Not long." Shyness still persevered with; but close-lipped, now.

"How long?"

"Not very. A month."

Smart kid, he thought. That keeps it all this side of sixteen. "We believe you have been indulging much longer than that."

"No, I haven't."

"Our doctor says you have."

"Well, I haven't." Less shyness now. More of defiance.

You cannot press a matter like this too far, even when you know subject is lying. Not when subject is sixteen and sitting in a headmistress's study. It can lead to hysterics—the headmistress rushing in—allegations against yourself and your lecherous mate. Blots on records, the case in hand ruined. Charges, possibly. No, you have to hold back. He said, quite gently,

"I believe your friend Deborah was in the same condition."

"Was she?"

"You didn't know?"

"No."

"We were hoping you might be able to tell us who she was—involved with. A man—men?"

"I don't know."

The shutter firmly down. Well, the sex-offense angle belonged to Johnnie Hogge. He changed the angle of approach.

"Paul Ross was with you in the Blue Grotto the other night, I'm told."

Her lovely eyes flickered briefly toward Sergeant Wimbush. "Yes," she said.

"I thought he was Deborah's boyfriend."

"He was."

"Wasn't it a bit soon after her death? I mean—aren't people usually—well—upset?"

"He was upset."

"But he was out dancing. With you."

"You don't have to go into a monastery."

"That's true."

"He wanted to—talk."

"To you."

"Yes. Well—Angie and me. We were her friends, too."

"He just wanted a shoulder to cry on."

"Yes."

"Uh-huh. I see. Well—thank you, miss. Somebody will be seeing you later, about the rape. As a matter of fact, I'm rather surprised to find you at school today."

"I'm working for A-levels."

"Ah. Don't want to fall behind. Very understandable. Commendable. Brave girl. All right, Sergeant—will you tell Miss Wellborn-Davit she is free to come back in? By the way, miss—you didn't ring me this morning, by any chance?"

"No. Why should I?"

"Why should you, indeed?"

The sergeant had opened the door. Miss Wellborn-Davit came in rapidly, beady-eyed like a black-haired hen puffed about the bosom with fluffed-up outrage. "Have you quite finished, Mr. Parsons?" she said.

"Quite finished, madam, thank you."

"Then you may return to your form room, Helen. Unless you would prefer to go home?"

"I'll go back to the form room, Miss Wellborn-Davit. Thank you."

"Off you go, then, dear. You really should have told me, you know. Or at least mentioned it to Miss Dawkins. If you don't feel up to it, you are free to go home, tell her."

"Thank you, Miss Wellborn-Davit." The girl got up, and was quietly gone. The sergeant, holding the door open for her, took in the clean scent of skin and hair as she passed close by, and felt genuine sorrow: for the danger to such lovely things of rape; for the fact that she was so far from virgin and so had destroyed his erotic dream. Very few men dream of whores. The dream of gentle guidance given to a virgin in black woolen stockings is in itself a yearning for lost innocence.

Miss Wellborn-Davit came with them, all the way to the steps, where, before they got into the car, the inspector made the obligatory farewell. "Well—good morning, madam. And thank you once again for your cooperation."

"Good morning, Mr. Parsons," she said. "One trusts that you have gathered all the information you require, it is rather disturbing for the girls to have the police back-and-forthing all the time. One is quite surprised that she does not appear to have told anybody about it."

"Perhaps she told her friends."

"If she had," said Miss Wellborn-Davit decidedly, "the school would be seething with it. One would certainly have known. But then, of course, some girls are too embarrassed by that sort of thing even to speak of it among themselves."

"Does she go home to lunch, do you know?"

"No. No, she lunches in the canteen. Very few of our girls do not."

"Thank you. Good morning again, madam. And—er—thank you."

They drove away, leaving the headmistress wondering vaguely why they should care where the child had lunch. Sergeant Wimbush said, as the inspector brought the car out from the school gates onto the road: "Do you think she was? Embarrassed?"

"Don't know. They're funny creatures, women."

"I thought you might lean on her a bit harder." There were many angles the inspector could have tested and explored, a wealth of skill in interrogation that he had not used.

"That was enough. We found out all we'd get for now—she's no downy innocent, she handled it well. Mark of the natural bent. Think we'll just put a tail on her, see if we've rattled her into something interesting."

"What kind of something?"

"Don't know. But I think they may be plying for hire. She may try to contact somebody."

"Good," said Wammo Wimbush, "because that's what I think. What time you want the tail on?" He was reaching for the radio mike.

"Now, I'd suggest. If she's rattled, she may skip lunch,

come trotting out. You'd better stay for now, point her out to him. Only keep out of sight. If she sees you, she'll pop back in, or something."

"What are you going to do?"

Pete grinned. "Find a nice cup of coffee. Then have a word with the lad."

"It's the rich what gets the pleasure," his legman said. He addressed the mike, summoning the tail.


It had been good thinking on the inspector's part. Young Helen did come out from the school at just after midday; which meant that she did not even wait for lunch. By this time, Parsons was at another school—St. Peter's Grammar School for Boys. Nowhere else in the town did the pupils, ranging from short and shrill to frighteningly large and hairy, wear a red jacket with gray piping, teamed with gray slacks. Nowhere else was Paul Ross among those who hollered a hymn every morning in a brawling cacophony stretched from treble to thunderous bass, with all the cracks and hootings in between. If some of the teachers ticced visibly, it was not because they existed precariously in a blackboard jungle; as boys go, these were relatively civilized. Those tics were the inevitable result of facing the sudden bay after a piano introduction at morning assembly, day after day, between the long holidays they needed to knit themselves together again.

Pete did not enter the school. He sat in his car, drawn up at the curb outside the gates, about fifty yards along and on the opposite side of the road. No point in setting another school up for chat, without reason; and boys, the inspector knew—after all, he used to be one—will rag unmercifully one of their number sent for to be interviewed by the police.

144

So he waited outside. If the lad stayed for a canteen lunch—well, then he'd go in; but if he ate at home, he would come out through those gates and could be quietly approached and spoken to discreetly in the car.

He did come. Boys and youths of all sizes came, and he among the last of them, walking subdued and alone where most were in groups, or at least in pairs, and inclined to skylarking. A loner, without doubt. Probably very high in the academic placings, with a leaning toward mathematics. Not, you would think, a lad ruled by the burgeoning penis. There were many who looked more sexually elastic, better suited to the seemingly randy lass who had been his girlfriend.

He came this way, which saved driving after him. Crossed the road and walked right by the car, the only lad who did. The policeman needed only to lean over, wind the window down, and speak through it. "Good morning, Mr. Ross. Can I talk to you a minute?"

"Er—" the lad said, taken by surprise. In this day of gay liberation, boys as well as girls need to be wary, hailed suddenly from a motor car. There was one standing opposite the school gates at this very moment, very gay indeed in down-at-heel shoes and a dirty raincoat, eyeing yearningly the emerging jailbait, pimples and all.

"Would you mind getting in for a moment?" The inspector opened the door. Obviously, the lad recognized him. Without a word he entered the car, closing the door behind him. Parsons said, smiling the soothing smile, "Well, now—how's life?"

"All right," the boy replied. That pale, self-guarded thin-pudding look had deepened. He said no more. The policeman spoke again.

"We had a phone call. Said you were seen with Debbie Hollowbone, going into the wood the night she died."

"I wasn't." A flat statement. And the attempt to unsettle by shock an abject failure. Nothing of emotion showed in the lad at all. The answer, in fact, killed the probe completely, as a dead bat drops the ball lifeless. And difficult to launch again, because the caller did not, in fact, give any name to the boy allegedly seen, or even a detailed description.

"When did you say you saw her last?"

"The day before."

"Uh-huh. Not at all on the day she died."

"No."

"You went dancing the following night. With her friends."

"Yes."

"Bit soon?"

Dead bat, all the way. "I'd have thought you'd have been upset."

"I was."

Nothing to be learned from this one if he didn't mean to tell you. No way to pressure him; and if there were, the harder the pressure, the thicker the layer of pudding he would present. After all, the inspector was here only on the strength of an anonymous phone call, in the belief that it never does any harm, when you have time for it, to stir everything up a bit. "All right," he said. "Off you go. Enjoy your lunch."

For the first time, the lad showed something of human reaction. A quick sideways flash of the eye betrayed surprise at the abrupt termination of the interview. Clearly, he had expected it to last longer. But he said nothing. Not even farewell. Simply opened the door in silence, got out, closed the door, and walked away.

Nothing so difficult, the inspector thought, watching him go, as trying to probe the minds of adolescents used to guarding secrets from parents and teachers and the enemy adult world. But the same rule applies to them as to anybody: The less they tell you, the more they have to hide.

# ·14·

It is not so unnoticeable as TV and the movies suggest, two men keeping obbo from a car, especially when the direct view of the area under observation is set in a street through which not much traffic passes. So Sergeant Wimbush, when the tail arrived in an innocuous vehicle, had him drive to where the gates of Queen Victoria's School are still visible, but from the busier main road. They were lucky to find a parking space, right where they needed it.

Helen came out alone, a few minutes after noon; so, Wammo Wimbush thought, she's in a hurry. Hurrying along, coming this way. He said to the tail, a Detective Constable Hannigan:

"That's her, look. Now don't cock it up—she should be coming back before two."

"Little cracker, ain't she?" said Detective Constable Hannigan. Another young man, with a young man's keen appetite.

"Never mind that—get moving."

"Not half."

The pretty thing passed by, other side of the busy street. Off went Constable Hannigan, keeping to this side, applying discretion without strain; so many people were about. She went straight down into the town center; straight through

147

the door that led to Roger Dunbutt's office, first floor of the building-society building.

Constable Hannigan followed. He knew—all policemen did—who dwelt up there, without need to consult the little brass plate screwed to the wall. Easy enough to dredge up a reason for calling in, something to do with some old lag. He opened the door to the outer office. Nobody here but the red-haired girl. He said: "Hi, Vera. Roger about?"

"He's got somebody in with him at the moment," she said.

"Anybody I know?"

"A schoolgirl. Very pretty." No envy in it. Rather, impressed admiration. She had a nice nature.

"Ah—right. I'll call in later. Be good." He closed the door and went downstairs, to lean upon a wall and wait.

Fat Roger, up in his office, had already asked, in a muffled and sweaty explosion, what the hell she was doing, calling here! She had already said, as explosively, that she had to see him, and he had hissed keep your voice down. She had said the police had been to see her again, and he had pulled out a handkerchief with which to dab his forehead and under-jowl and said why? What did they want?

"I was raped," she said.

"Raped? What do you mean, raped? When?"

"Last night. In the park."

"Raped? Who raped you?"

"Two fellers. They examined me."

"Examined you?"

"The police. The doctor—he examined me. He told them I'd been at it a long time."

"They didn't—you didn't tell them anything?"

"Of course I didn't. But—they'll be coming again. This

one—there are two of them—wanted to know about Paul and Debbie and—"

"Did he say his name?"

"Parsons. He's an inspector. The other one's name is—I can't remember—he's a sergeant—they've been before. And there's another one coming to see me about the rape thing—"

"Did they say so?"

"Yes—and last night I saw one called Sergeant Hogge. And the doctor and a woman policeman and—"

"All right, all right," said Roger. Fat men have pink lips that go moist and loosen under stress. "All right—all right—listen—don't ever come here. I told you—you're never to come here—"

"I couldn't phone—you said we mustn't phone—" Because the girl listens in.

"I know, I know. Don't phone, either. And keep your voice down. Go back to school—don't say anything—"

"I'll have to say something, won't I? Old Wellborn-Davit knows about—last night—and she'll tell the teachers—and the police, they'll be coming—to the house—and my mum and dad will be—if he tells them I've been doing it a lot—they'll *kill* me."

"Only the rape. Only tell them about the rape." Not a word of sympathy for the foul deed committed upon her, you'll notice.

"I don't know if I can—I don't know if they'll let me—you don't know what they're like—"

Oh yes, he did. He'd worked close by them for long enough. He said, with forehead glistening, "Just don't—babble—that's all. Don't say anything about anything, only the rape. I'll come to the door with you." He went all the way to the outer door, holding her arm lightly, and said in a voice bluff and hearty: "Don't you worry about a thing, my dear, I shall take care of the matter."

All this for the benefit of the red-haired girl, who clacked at her typewriter thinking: I wish I looked like that, she's made old Slobber-Chops sweat, look. Randy old basket. Not that he's ever tried it on me, but they're all alike.

Constable Hannigan fell in again behind Helen when she emerged, and followed her back to the school. Because a man cannot be in two places at once, he did not see Roger Dunbutt come out a minute or two behind her and scurry away to a telephone booth in the post office nearby. He needed to speak with Alderman Withers again, and did not favor being listened in to by the red-haired girl.

Alderman Withers was at home—he enjoyed a substantial lunch taken quite early, with a nap to follow—and his side of this conversation was very brief indeed. He snapped: "Get off the line. I'll see you at the exhibition."


By the time Pete Parsons and Wammo Wimbush arrived at the exhibition, they had attended an after-lunch meeting in the Assistant Chief Constable's office, together with Superintendent Ted Churchyard. You could almost call it a courtesy meeting, the field workers' deferential bow to the man who carries the ultimate can. Mind you, if they failed to offer the nod at least once a day, there'd have been bum-kicking about.

Ted Churchyard had not been idle during the morning. He had conducted a press conference, affixed a strip of sticking plaster to a knee that went out of control and bashed itself upon the edge of a desk, and spoken on the telephone to Ellie, relict of Albert Fish. Could she tell him, he asked, the name of Albert's bank?

She was very brusque. "Why?"

"Routine, madam, in a murder case," he told her.

She positively snapped. "Well, I don't know. Don't know if he even had a bank."

"We have reason to believe he had been spending rather freely of late—"

"Not on me, he hadn't."

"Ah. Perhaps not. But certainly in other directions."

"I don't know anything about that. I was his wife, not his bank manager." And she hung up.

Mr. Churchyard reported this, of course, in the Assistant Chief Constable's office. The great man said, "Uh-huh. Awkward lady, is she?"

"Yes, sir. It's written all over her."

"Well—there are more ways of killing a cat." More ways, he meant, than bashing into the uncooperative. The law entitles the policeman to bash mentally, and he knows how. But he knows, too, that there is no need to put yourself to all the aggro when other, less arduous, means are available. Senior policemen—bank managers—they all know each other in a smallish town. Share the same clubs, play golf, attend the odd function together. Every manager is on terms with the managers of other branches, in the city as well as the town, and the same goes for building societies. And every bank and building society has a telephone. What a boon that instrument is.

"I've already started killing this one, sir. Barclays in Broad Street—he's got five thousand in."

"Five thousand. Not bad. Lucky feller."

"Very lucky, for a caretaker. All deposited over the last year. What's more, it's a joint account. Him and her."

"Uh-huh. And she didn't know? Odd."

"Odd."

"Did she have money? When they got married—did she

put it in a joint account then? Love's young dream—what's yours is mine, what's mine is yours?"

"She was a school cook."

"Uh-huh. You need to flog a lot of rice for that much money. Married before? Did her first husband die warm?" Kite-flying again; not really believing his was the first mind to wander this way.

"It's been building up over the year—a few hundred here, few there. Irregular deposits." The superintendent brought out a list and read from it: sums deposited and dates. The bank manager was an old friend.

"Interesting. You'll be following it up?" Again—not a real question. Nobody thought it was. Courtesy between senior professionals, is all.

"Straightaway, sir."

Not a vast fortune, £5,000; but interesting when a man saves more than he is earning. The Chief passed on, to Chief Inspector Parsons and his favorite oppo. "And you, Mr. Parsons, I take it will be pursuing the other matter?"

"I will, sir."

"Yes. Well—so long as the two cases can be handled at once, you might as well carry on."


Pete Parsons and Wammo Wimbush did not even know there was an exhibition. They found out when they arrived at Roger Dunbutt's office, smiled pleasantly on the red-haired girl, and said they'd like to see him.

"He's not here," she said. "He's getting the exhibition ready."

"Is he?" said Pete. "What exhibition?"

"The Photographic Society. At the Presley Hall."

"Jolly good." Oo, she thought, he does have a nice smile. So does the other one. Makes my belly quiver. "Left you to mind the shop, has he?"

"Don't suppose much'll happen. It never does." She sounded quite depressed about it. Well, until the blood dies down in the veins, it's not much of a life, typing and answering the telephone and making tea. Not much of a life after that, either, but a body can settle to it better. She had some way to go, if the smiles of policemen still put a quiver into her belly. And she said herself that they did, so there is no reason to doubt it.

They had left the car in a park attached to a super-market, and it was not worth getting it out to seek new parking at the Presley Hall, named not for Elvis but for an Edwardian town benefactor noted for charitable works who beat his wife and terrified children, but very privily. As they walked the few blocks, Pete said, "I didn't know Roger is a photo buff."

"Course he is," said Wammo. "Big noise in the society, hon. sec. or something; I used to belong myself. Old Withers used to belong, used to be chairman. Might still be, I dunno. I gave it up, couldn't afford it."

"Any good? Old Roger?"

"Yeah, not bad. Landscapes, mostly. Portraits of his old mum with her teeth out, shawl on her bonce. Title: 'Serenity.' 'Eventide.' 'In Old Portugal.' That sort of thing."

They arrived at the Presley Hall within minutes of Al-derman Withers, who would never have lingered had he seen them coming. He had no intention of lingering anyway, he was not here for the pleasure. But he had to find out what, if any-thing, had restarted Roger's panic and sent him scrambling for the oft-forbidden telephone.

There were women about, affixing prints to the bare walls. But the table at which Roger was arranging hardware exhibits stood in the middle of the big hall, and if the joviality with which he beamed good-afternoons toward them sat a bit awkwardly on the alderman, they were far enough away and too preoccupied with happy chat to notice. He approached Roger's table and said, keeping his beam going and his voice low:

"What do you want?"

Roger told him: about the girl's having been raped, the police visits—all of it. "She's panicking," he said, looking not far from panic himself.

"Did anybody see her with you?"

"My girl. Only my girl."

"Smile. Smile," said Alderman Withers, setting an example. He picked up one of the exhibits, a long telephoto lens; examined it ostentatiously. "Just keep your head, that's all. Just keep your head." And then he looked up, to find the two policemen bearing down. "Ah," he said, the beam faltering, "here come—ah."

Pete Parsons spoke cheerily, when he came within range. "Afternoon, Mr. Withers, Roger." And, glancing around the hall: "Looks like a good exhibition."

"Good afternoon, Inspector," the alderman said, beaming hard. "Yes. Yes. I just slipped in to—er—just to see our Roger wasn't—mucking it all up, you know. Ha ha. Yes. I must—er—be off. See you later, Roger, I'll be here for the opening. Yes. Good day, gentlemen."

"Good day," they said; and when he had bustled away, Pete addressed Roger. "Didn't know you were into photography, Roj. Are you exhibiting?"

"Yes," said Roger. "Mm. Well—just a couple of landscapes. And a portrait. Of my mother. Over there." He pointed; dropped his fat finger. "Oh—they're not up yet."

"I'll have to come back, have a look at 'em. When do you open?"

"Tomorrow. Ten o'clock."

"Uh-huh." The inspector had picked up that big tele-photo lens standing like a lighthouse amid smaller lenses, exposure meters, various old and new cameras, and bits of equipment on the table. "This is a big bugger. I'm no bottle at this caper, seem to cut all the heads off. There's a girl called Helen Jonas, Roj, visited you at lunchtime."

"Jonas?" said Roger. "Helen Jonas? Oh—yes. Yes."

"What did she want?"

Roger was not thinking very well. Had his wits been bounding nimbly, he might have picked the whole ambience up and used it, said she was modeling for a portrait or something, called in to say she couldn't keep an appointment. God knows, she was pretty enough, a natural for innocent girlhood stuff, bit of chiffon draped artistically over the head and shoulders bare. But he didn't think of it. He was badly shaken by their presence, and their knowing she called. He said, "She was—concerned—about one of our clients. A relative." And because a suddenly rattled liar is impelled, somehow, to embroider, he added: "Her—er—uncle."

"Uncle?" said Pete. "Has she got a bent uncle? What's got her worried, then? Going wrong again, is he?"

"I—can't tell you that."

"No." Well, he couldn't. Strictly private, the traffic between himself, his office, and his clients. No business of the police. "What's his name?"

"I can't tell you that, either."

Pete grinned. "Didn't think you would. Did she tell you she was raped last night?"

"Yes. Yes. Terrible."

Wammo Wimbush spoke. "There's an awful lot of it about."

"I don't think," said Roger, reaching for dignity, "it's a joking matter."

"You have to giggle a bit," said Wammo, "or you go barmy."

"Saw her myself this morning." Pete was speaking again. "Well, we both did."

"Ah," said Roger. "About the rape?"

"No. Another matter. Well—we'll let you go on, Roj, you're doing a great job. We'll just wander around for a minute, have a look at what you've got on the walls."

"Yes," said Roger. "Right."

They wandered, while he resumed his setting out of exhibits on the table, arranging and rearranging, judging for effect. In a short while they cried a farewell and left. Before they were clear of the building, Pete was saying:

"What do you make of that?"

"Sweating," said Wammo. "Written all over him. He's got the breeze up his kilt."

"Good lad, you noticed. Now why would that be?" They were going down the steps now, back into the street.

"Course, he may just be sickening or something."

"He looked as though he'd got it. Sounded as if it had caught him by the cobblers."

"That'll make anybody sweat, a good grip on the cobblers."

"See that doorway over there?" said the senior man. "Go and hide in it, see what happens."

Privately, Wammo believed that the better idea was to go back in, gather Roger, and really lean. They should have leaned there and then, in his opinion, while they had the lad sweating and clearly floundering. Nothing hard and fast to hit

156

him with, but the way to find out why fat jowls should quiver shinily is to lean. However, his not to reason. The man says hide in a doorway, go hide in a doorway. "What are you going to do?" he asked.

"Cogitate," said Pete. "Better give it five, ten minutes. See you back at the factory. Anything urgent, ring in."

# ·15·

Alderman Withers went straight home. He had only just left it; but he needed to be back there, where the stiffening was. He told that stiffening all about Roger, the girl's visit to him, and the sudden arrival of police at the exhibition. She asked,

"What did they want to see him about?"

"I don't know," he told her. "I couldn't very well stick there, could I? I had to leave."

"It may just have been routine business. They deal with him a lot, don't they?" Then the telephone rang. She answered it. A brief call. When she replaced the receiver, she said, "Dunbutt. Calling from the post office. They wanted to know why the girl visited, he said it was about a client. Her uncle."

"Uncle? What uncle?"

"The fool says he didn't have a chance to think, he just said it."

"She hasn't got an uncle. Has she? Not with Roger. They'll find out, won't they?"

"Be quiet. Let me think." She sat for a while with corrugated brow in her fine armchair in that handsome room, he pacing the carpet; pausing by the drinks cabinet to pour himself a Scotch. At length, she said, "We'll have to get on to him again. Will he be down there all the afternoon?"

"I don't know. Yes. Well—if he's getting the exhibition ready—"

"You'd better go back."

"I don't want—the police may still be—"

"They're not. He said they left."

"They may come back—"

"For God's sake," she snapped, "stiffen yourself up. We can't ring him there. Nobody's going to think it funny, you popping in and out, you're chairman, aren't you? They'd think it more funny if you didn't, annual exhibition and all. All the stuff's got to go, he's got to destroy it. Make sure he does."

"Fish—Fish—"

"Listen to me!" Come stiffly upright, eyes glittering, she really was a formidable lady, in twin set and cultured pearls. "If everything is destroyed, nobody has any evidence."

"There are prints—"

"Not with anybody who'd dare show them. So long as everybody keeps their mouths shut, there's nothing to connect anybody with anything."

"They may not keep—the police—Roger and the girl—"

Yes, yes, yes—she knew, she knew, and she didn't like it any more than he did. But one thing at a time, and the first was to keep this oaf from gibbering. She barked, as he went in to the bottle again: "No more of that! I need you sober."

He put the Scotch down. "An uncle? What made him— he must be mad—"

"Never mind that—get down there. *Everything* to be destroyed, soon as possible."


It did not take Pete Parsons long to seek out Sergeant Johnnie Hogge, when he got back to the station, and to say to him where he sat chomping cod and chips well swamped with tomato catsup:

"You got the rape job, Johnnie?"

"Yup," said Johnnie. "Why?"

"When are you seeing her?"

"Going to the house, five o'clock."

"Late as that?"

"No rush, we've got the herberts. All I need's her statement. I'd a full book for today before this one came in." *Crackle* went his fine, tough teeth, destroying that dark brown and thickly battered piece lurking at the nether end of canteen-fried cod. Some say this is the best bit. Some say it tastes like fried grasshopper. "Her parents work, they don't get home till five."

Again, it came to the inspector that somebody—the girl, surely, and Mum—might have been expected to take today off. He said as much. The cod-eating sergeant said, a finger in his mouth to detach a bone from his teeth:

"The mum rang. Thed the girl wanted to go to thchool, thed they thought it betht to carry on ath normal, if thatth what thshe wanted."

His finger came out all wet and shiny. Not a pretty sight. The inspector said, "Can you give 'em a ring?"

"Not till they get home." A man can talk quite clearly through cod, provided he has no finger stuck in his mouth; although this, too, is not necessarily a pretty sight. "Don't know where they work."

The inspector did not say well, you should bloody well have found out. No reason why the sergeant should, he was concerned only with getting the girl's statement and having her parents there while he did it. "Do me a favor—ring 'em before you go, ask if they've got a relation—an uncle—no, just say a relation—in touch with Roger Dunbutt."

"Roger?" They all knew Roger, around here. "One of his clients?"

"Could be. That's what I want to find out. Be discreet, huh? Just ask, let me know the answer. Say you're ringing to confirm that they'll be there before you set out, don't say you're on about uncle."

"Will do." Sergeant Hogge pushed aside his cod plate and reached for the prunes and custard, sucking his lips with anticipatory relish, grease all over his chin. The entire family ate like that, both feet in the trough. This one showed no interest in why he should be asked to ask the question, but he'd do the job. Pete left him to it. No point in needlessly risking flying custard. He was downstairs and on his way to check with the computer—he couldn't remember a Jonas, but there might be one; although, of course, an uncle can have the mother's maiden name. Never mind, worth a check—when a man stepping out of the radio room said, "Ah—just the bloke, been buzzing your office. Wammo Wimbush is asking for you, on the walkie-talkie."

Wammo Wimbush's call was delayed by the fact that his own personal radio had gone on the blink. The damn things are always doing it. The doorway in which Pete had urged him to hide was perfect. He did not need even to lurk in it, because it gave directly into a bare stone hall, with bare stone stairs to one side and an old-fashioned cage-type lift serving offices above. Nobody about, everybody working or at lunch. He stayed very happily, for something less than the five, ten minutes Pete had suggested as lurking time. Fine view, nobody to eye him suspiciously as shopkeepers are wont to do, when you stand for too long flattened in their doorways. You cannot really blame them.

Four minutes elapsed before Roger emerged, something

furtive about his glancing right and left as he hurried down the steps and along to the post office, within sight between a department store and an office block just down the street. This is when Sergeant Wimbush reached for his pocket radio and found it on the blink.

He might have repaired it, given a screwdriver and a small flat surface to work on, but he had no screwdriver, and no flat surface. He said, "Sod it," and shook it at his ear, his eyes on the fat man entering one of the phone booths that stand outside the post office, littered with old soggy chip papers and the normal who's who of who loves whom in black felt-tipped lettering. No sense in possibly blowing cover by following him; short of tugging the door open and inserting an ear, there was no way of telling whom he was ringing and what was said.

One thing was for sure: Pete was no mug. Rattle 'em, and watch. The bugger had come out, sure enough, to scurry to an impersonal phone rather than use the one inside, where a person may be listened to, or overheard. That says something.

Roger was not lingering. Whomever he rang did not enjoy for long the benefit of his conversation. Already he had put the phone down and was hurrying back, to reenter the Presley Hall. Do I go now? the sergeant asked himself. Back to the factory, to tell Pete he was right? Or do I stay?

I stay. Should be a beat man along soon, complete with a walkie-talkie.

There was. Usually, when you want one, you can't find one. As he loomed past the door, Wammo popped out and said, "Oi, lad, come in here."

The policeman knew him. A bright boy, he stepped inside without a word. Not until then did he speak. "Hello, Sarge. What's up?"

"How's your walkie-talkie?"

"All right. How's yours?"

"On the sodding blink. Hand over."

Several more minutes of squawk and splutter went by before the station located Inspector Parsons. He came on and said through it all:

"Wammo? Where are you? Over."

"Where you told me to be. Over."

"Oh yes—Dobson's doorway. Any joy? Over."

"He came out. Made a phone call, along at the post office. Couldn't report before, my walkie's kaput. Hang on—hang on—here comes the alderman. Withers. He's going in. Looks very sweaty. In a' hurry."

Alderman Withers' car had appeared, and had swung into one of those parking spaces that are vacant so rarely—oh, so rarely—within walking distance of where you want to be. A car edged out—he swung in—voilà! Almost opposite of where the policemen were tucked away, the alderman alighted, half trotted to and up the Presley Hall steps, vanished inside. The sergeant spoke on.

"Want me to go in, see if he's nattering with Roger? Over."

"No." Withers? Something bent involving Withers? Possibly, something bent can involve anybody. But not likely. Why shouldn't the man come back to the exhibition? Big event in the photo society year; and after all— "You said he was chairman, didn't you? Over."

"Yeah. Over."

"Well, then. Over."

"He's sweating. Over."

"Who's with you? Over."

"The beat lad. Over."

"Hodgekiss," said the copper. "Dave Hodgekiss."

"Who is it? Over."

"Hodgekiss," said Wammo. "Dave Hodgekiss. Over."

"All right. Want to come back? Over."

"Up to you. I could do with a bit of lunch. Over."

"Right. Tell your lad to keep obbo, you know, walk up and down the street, call in if anything interesting happens. Over."

"Uh-huh. Will do. Over."

"See you, then. Over and out."

The conversation was over. Wammo handed the uniform man's radio back to him and said, "Do you know Roger Dunbutt?"

"Everybody knows Roger Dunbutt."

"Did you hear what Mr. Parsons said?"

"Was that Mr. Parsons?"

"Stick to this street. Keep obbo on the hall. If and when Mr. Dunbutt comes out, buzz in. If you see anything interesting, buzz in. Right?"

"Ten-four," said the constable, a devotee of American cop series. He added, "I'm off at two."

"Lucky old you. You could cop a bit of overtime, and cover yourself with glory."


Inside the hall, Alderman Withers had approached Roger, who by now was attaching prints to the wall with Bluetack, an invaluable substance leaving no mark. The women club members were in a small kitchen that lies tucked away behind a door marked "Private," where they were brewing tea and nibbling at dainty sandwiches with the crusts cut off, all wrapped in paper napkins, a spare one to dab the delicate lips with. Well, you don't want people to think you live like pigs. The fact that they were in there enabled the men to converse with relative freedom, albeit with eyes that tended to glance about, warily.

164

Roger, in a fresh outbreak of sweat, had said when the alderman reappeared that he should not have come back. The alderman had said that he had to. Everything was to be destroyed, and he couldn't ring here because you never know, with all these women about, who is listening. Roger said you don't know who's watching, either; and the alderman said urgently: nobody, you're getting yourself into a panic; and anyway, as chairman of the club, there was nothing odd about his calling in from time to time, to see how it was all shaping. Roger then said,

"We can't do it now—my girl's there."

"Can't you get her out of it?"

"Not while I'm here—she's the only one in the office, she'd think it funny."

"Better get back. Send her out for something."

"We'll have to move all the furniture."

"What time does she go home?"

"Five-thirty."

"All right—all right." It would have to wait until five-thirty, then. They couldn't hump furniture with the red-haired girl about. And the stuff could not be destroyed in the office. No stove, to poke it all into, and it certainly must not be shoved in a wastepaper basket. It would have to be transported: to a fire, or dumped in the river, well weighted. "Half past five. I'll meet you. Outside your office." And the alderman took himself off.

Constable Hodgekiss saw him go and radioed the fact in to the station, where other things were beginning to happen. For one of which: Mrs. Ellie Fish was being delivered by squad car, into the care of Superintendent Ted Churchyard.

# ·16·

Most cases begin to open when somebody does something absolutely stupid, and when money is involved, the action is invariably rooted in greed, exacerbated often by fear that Authority—the police—will find out that it exists; and that this will result not only in the loss of it, but in spurring Authority on to other discoveries. Greed and panic combined clear more cases than are solved by brilliant detective work. This is why so many policemen spend so much time lurking out of sight, watching to see what people are going to do, once they have been unsettled.

In this case, Mrs. Ellie Fish was not even suspect. Nor was her foolish action spied upon by the police. It was the manager of that Barclays bank called earlier by Ted Churchyard who called back later. Mr. Churchyard said, "Keep her there in your office, I'll have her picked up. Nice work, Edgar, thank you," he said.

So this public-spirited and canny man enticed her into his office, saying that he must get head office clearance before paying out such a large sum in cash; and he even managed to keep her there, in spite of her bristled nervous condition, by soothingly outlining various investment opportunities while waiting, he said, for head office to ring back. And then two plainclothes policemen arrived, and ran her in.

She objected, of course she did; but she was caught, in

the figurative sense only, with her pants down. Now she sat stiffly on the nasty little chair facing the inhospitable table in the least hospitable interview room. On the only other chair, behind the table, sat Superintendent Churchyard, folded down with his knees tucked out of the way. Chief Inspector Pete Parsons leaned against a wall. Churchyard had been doing the talking. He was saying again what he had said many times before.

"Where did all this money come from, Mrs. Fish?"

She snapped. Exactly as she had throughout. "That's my business."

Surprising how many people appear sincerely to believe that however dubious the circumstances surrounding them, their business is nobody else's business. "It's our business, too," said Ted Churchyard. "Isn't it? I say it again—it's a great deal of money, spread over several accounts." He had heard from his team. There were other accounts, in the city. Almost doubled the money. Now why would a man like Albert go all the way to the city, to establish and feed joint accounts? "Are you telling me it was saved in one year out of Albert's wages? Housekeeping, rent, rates out of it? Income known, normal council rate. We can't believe that, can we? Not even if you are working. Are you working?"

Chin up, eyes glitteringly hostile, she said, "I do voluntary work."

"Uh-huh. Where?"

"The Family Planning Clinic. Part time. Two afternoons a week."

"Do you get paid?"

"No."

"Well, then. How do you account for this money?"

"I want to see my solicitor," she said, and shut her mouth like a snapping turtle.

"That won't be possible."

"I have my rights—"

There is a simple way for the police to deny a suspect his right to have a solicitor present during interview. The law qualifies the right. Mr. Churchyard had passed this way often. Every seasoned officer has. "It would impede our investigations."

"What investigations? You've got no right—"

"Oh yes, we have. Forgery is a serious offense."

"It's me money—he left it—I'm his wife—"

"Uh-huh." So why didn't you wait for the will to be proved, why didn't you arrange an advance against it, if you were skint? Because a will is public, because all this lolly probably doesn't feature on any will. Because you are a stupid woman, and greedy, and scared. "Let's start again, shall we? Why did you forge Albert's signature on this check?"

That is what she did. Made a clumsy fist of it, too. Presented it against the joint account, trying to clear it completely on two signatures, one of which was very wobbly. Nobody was fooled for a second.

"I didn't forge anything. He left it signed."

Stupid. Stupid woman. Half an hour they'd been at it, she denying the obvious. Ted Churchyard sighed, and began to unfold himself. When he was on his considerable feet, he said, "All right, Mrs. Fish. You're being very silly. We will be holding you here, of course."

"What for?"

"You'll have time to work that out. Mr. Parsons, perhaps you will ask a big fat policeman to take the lady away."

The policeman came. Not fat, not very big as policemen go, but of adequate size and weight to escort her down to one of the underground cells. On the way to the superintendent's office, Pete Parsons said,

"Think she had anything to do with Albert's death?"

"Could be," said Mr. Churchyard. "Wanted all the gelt for herself. Only snag: You'd have thought she'd have talked him into leaving a check or two signed before he was knocked off. And she was in Derby, I've had it checked."

"Could she have had it done on contract?"

"Doubt if she's got the connections. Or the brains."

"Mm. Don't see Albert being mug enough to sign blank checks for her. He wouldn't be that stupid."

"Well, he didn't, did he? She tried to forge it."

"What about the city account?"

"That's a building society. She meant to clear that too, no doubt. We'll find out."

Sergeant Johnnie Hogge came from the CID room as they passed. He said, "Ah—Pete—just on the way to see you. Rang the Jonases. They haven't got anybody mixed up with Dunbutt. Sounded a bit indignant when I told 'em what he does, they didn't even know his name."

"Right, Johnnie, ta," said Pete. "That's what I thought."

"Anytime," the sergeant said, and took himself back into the CID room. As the two detectives moved on, the long tall one said, "What's that about, then?" And, when Pete had sketched the picture for him in the time it took to mount the stairs: "Dunbutt, eh? Reckon he's into something bent, then?"

"Say the radar's started giving blips. Know something? My girl case and Albert—I'm beginning to think they may be coming together."

"Uh-huh."

"And I'm wondering if our Roger isn't in there some-where. Likewise, the Fish lady."

"Come back to square one. I'm stuck on it."

"Helen Jonas—raped last night—rushing off to Roger this morning. We ask him why, he feeds us a lot of bollix about

169

her uncle. Quack says she's been at it like a rattlesnake. Her and the Hollowbone girl. So we have two birdies—and maybe the other two, for all I know—shagging away and nobody getting pregnant. Albert's wife does voluntary work. Family Planning Clinic. Albert was caretaker at the school, he knew all the girls—my little dead one, her mates, and all. Helen was one of her close mates. Roger got him the job." He paused and looked surprised as the radar blipped again. "With the backing of Alderman Withers. And Withers has been blue-arsing in and out of the Presley Hall. Sweating, Wammo says."

"Withers?" said Ted Churchyard, dubiously. "Getting a bit high on the municipal list, ain't we? Where is Wammo?"

"Downstairs, catching up on a bit of paper."

"Mm. Well—all that's your pigeon, I've only got Albert. What do you want to do?"

"Catch up on my own paper. Chew this lot over while I do it. Don't need me, do you?"

"No. I'll be working the lady over again, but I don't need you for that. Better let me know where I can reach you, if you're going out."

"Will do," said Pete, and he took himself down the stairs again, to his own room, from where he phoned Suzie, only because he felt like doing it, and then settled with no pleasure to his pile of paperwork.


All this time, and for some time after, the young policeman left to keep obbo on Helen had been sitting in his car, still parked by arrangement with the traffic warden in that main road slot from which he could see the school gates. Soon after three forty-five, girls began to emerge, she among them with her two friends. They came this way, turning left along the main road.

Again: Only in movies and television fantasies can a car nose out and follow, without being noticed, suspects proceeding at walking pace, in any kind of road. Certainly here, where traffic flows thick, the honking of irate horns from other impeded cars will blow gaff, if nothing else does. This policeman, knowing it well, stepped out and proceeded on foot.

He need not have bothered, they did nothing in any way naughty. Nothing remarkable at all. The plump one, the other pretty one, halted at a bus stop and remained there together. The one he was detailed to follow walked on, filly-fresh and fit to be dreamed about. He followed her with great pleasure all the way home, where she used her key and vanished.

He found a quiet corner and made his report by walkie-talkie. Extreme range, but Pete could make sense of it. They put the call through to him in his office. The radio room is all knitted in to the intercom. It saves a lot of rushing about. "All right, lad," he said, "you might as well jack it in—I don't think she'll be going out again." A fair bet, she was booked to see Johnnie Hogge in half an hour. He added, "Over," to start the squawk again. It said, faintly: "Right. Erspitzell skreek crackle. Over and out. Yeeurkk." And it was gone.

Pity the shadowing officer cannot follow right on the heels. Had this one been able to listen to the girlishly overwrought conversation, he might have injected a little more meat into his report. He would not have understood it—they were very guarded, the whispering centered on things he knew nothing about—but he would certainly have gathered that they were in a condition of high excitement, and have passed the fact on. Pity, too, that he could not follow Helen into her home, to hear the phone call she made before her parents came in—first her mother, and then her father, left work early to support her in her talk with the police.

She said, "Paul?"

"Yes," said the phone, guardedly.

"It's me—Helen. Can you talk?"

"What about?" Nothing at all given away.

"The police came to see me—at school—not about the rape, they're coming at five about that. The good-looking one, Parsons his name is. He keeps coming, he keeps asking questions."

"What questions?"

"Well—you know—I told you—and now he was asking about you—"

"Me? What about me?"

"He wanted to know what we were doing together in the Blue Grotto—I've got to go—my mum's coming—" She put the phone down as her mother stepped into the front hall, crying, "Are you there, dear?" "Yes, Mum," she said. "I was just going to put the kettle on."

At about this time, Pete Parsons was sitting with Wammo Wimbush in the canteen, and they were drinking tea out of the thick white cups that policemen prefer, because they do not crush in the grip. They were also eating, two big chocolate biscuits each out of individual wrappers that had a Funny Bunny printed on them. Send three of these wrappers together with your check or postal order for £2, and you get a real Funny Bunny in super-luxurious fluffed 100% Nylotex.

They were also talking, these two big men, and had been since Pete poked his head into the CID room and said, "Cuppa, Wam? I'm just going up." Now he was saying:

"So it looks to me as if you got it right first time."

"I could have told you that," said Wammo. "Well, I did, didn't I?"

172

"Hawking it. Sex caper. Our little Debbie and the Jonas girl."

"And the others, I wouldn't be surprised." Wammo was wearing the touch of smugness that comes upon the junior when he has shown the senior who ought to be wearing oak leaves on the shoulder.

"You're probably right there, too." Pete accepted the smugness with the equanimity of him who knows that by the time the other bloke has his oak leaves, he himself may well be wielding the Field Marshal's baton. "So who's been shagging them? Roger, for one?"

"I've often wondered if Roger's queer. Never married, has he?"

"Could be. Could be bi. Could be just starved, buys it where he can get it. Aging singles go a bit kinky, they favor little girls."

"So what do you reckon? Albert able to sound out the talent, sorted this little lot and passed 'em on?"

"Passed 'em to more than just Roger, if that was the way of it."

"Withers?"

"Could be. Delicate, if it is."

"They put Albert in there, didn't they?"

"And Albert's dead."

"With a lot of bread stashed. Which his old lady knew about."

"Yes. And she works at the birth-control clinic. You finished?"

"More or less." Wammo drained his cup.

"What do you say we go and lean on Roger a little?"

"Why don't we lean on the old lady?"

"Ted's handling that."

"Ready when you are." Down with the cup, up with the

body, the mind within thinking: We should have done a bit of leaning long ago.

They passed down the stairs, back to ground level, where Pete said: "Nothing in from the lad at the Presley Hall?"

"Nope."

"Raise him, huh? Just to check. I'll nip up and tell Ted we're going out."

The sergeant peeled off, into the radio room. His superior went up the stairs to the superior office of his superior, who agreed that leaning upon Roger might be a good thing to do, and gave the project his blessing. Down went Pete again, to find his legman waiting in the hall. Wammo said,

"Raised him. Nothing. Roger's still inside. I said we were coming down."

"Good," said Pete, and they started for the door; but the man in the reception booth—it's an office, really, glassed in—took the telephone from his ear and called across: "Wanted on the blower, Mr. Parsons." All outside calls were coming in to here at the moment, while the switchboard WPC quaffed tea and wondered whether a Funny Bunny might not be an idea, at £2, for a bug-eyed but, the clinic said, not seriously subnormal nephew for Christmas.

Pete leaned in at the inquiries window to take the call. "Chief Inspector Parsons," he said.

A little high voice came into his ear. "I saw Debbie Hollowbone going into the woods. With a boy."

"Are you—er—" Boy? Girl? Dwarf with malformed larynx? "You rang before—"

The voice was not listening, it was running on. "His name's Paul Ross."

"And what's your name?"

But the caller was gone. Pete said as he handed the phone back: "Ringing from a booth?"

"Uh-huh," the policeman said. You can always tell, by the *beep-beep-beep* when you pick up your instrument and the *thunk* as the money goes down. No way of tracing a booth call, so into the great unknown went the little high voice.

"Anybody I know?" Wammo asked as they left the building; and Pete told him what the little voice said as they walked down to the town center. Not worth taking a car, it isn't far off, and parking an increasing problem. Saturation point cannot be far off. Matters ease for the evening once the homing chaos is over; but this was five o'clock, with the rush time just beginning.

They walked on, and the next thing that happened was farce. Pure farce—which they appreciated when they caught up with it, but not fully because they were not actually present throughout. By the time they arrived, the active element was over. A pity, they would so have enjoyed it.

Some say a tittering Fate arranges these things. Some say the gods do it. Some maintain that it is mere accident, like the creation of the world and evolution, because there is no God, singular or plural. Whatever the rights of it, this would probably never have happened had they not met Roger's red-haired girl coming street-dressed from the office, which they had to pass en route for the Presley Hall. But for this they would have called in upstairs, in case he had returned; and there he would have been, with no chance to dig and delve, or caught just as he was beginning. But they stopped to speak with her. Wammo, who fancied her rather, bullied off and kept the action.

"Hello. Where are you bound for?"

"Home." She spoke with the winsome eye flutter of the girl who fancies them both at once. "Mr. Dunbutt's given me half an hour off."

"That's nice. Is he in there?"

"Yes. He just came back. With Mr. Withers. Something private."

"Ah. What?"

"He didn't say."

"Just something private."

"Well—yes. It must be, he said I could go home"

"Good. Enjoy yourself. What are you doing this evening?"

Hope sprang. Stomach and lashes fluttered together. "Nothing, really. Only watching telly."

"I'll be thinking of you."

"Ah," she said. "Yes. Good." And she went her way.

"You rotten bastard," said Pete Parsons.

"I know." The sergeant stood back, elaborately waving his hand toward the entrance to the building. "After you."

"Hang on. Here comes a copper."

PC Dave Hodgekiss, well up by now on overtime, was approaching from across the street. Remarkable, how the traffic slowed for him. "He's in there, Mr. Parsons," he said. "Alderman Withers called back for him at the hall, they got here five minutes ago. I buzzed the station; they said you were on the way down."

"Good lad," said Pete. "You'll go a long way."

"That'll make a change." The policeman returned grin for grin as he said it. "I'm sick to death of this bloody street."

"We going in, then?" asked Wammo.

"Hang about," said Pete. "Let Mr. Withers finish first. Stick around, Dave—Dave, is it?—I may need you. Let's wait in the hallway."

The constable would not have followed the reasoning— he didn't even know what it was all about—but Wammo did. An alderman can be dangerous, and nobody had valid reason for leaning on this one. Nor could the man to be leaned on be

176

leaned on in his company. Wait here, then, until the danger man left. Easy enough, if they came out together, to say, "Evening. Mr. Dunbutt, may we have a private word?" That way, if the danger man is bent, you may unsettle him without risking complaint—directed to the very top brass, in person. And you have the desired subject on his own, rattled by the mere fact of your appearing to snatch him away.

So the three policemen stood about in the hallway, while upstairs, the farce was already rolling.

# ·17·

After the red-haired girl had left, Roger Dunbutt said to Alderman Withers, "We'll have to move the desk and the filing cabinet."

"Lock the door," said the alderman. "We don't want people blundering in."

So Roger locked the door and led the way into the inner office, going straight to the filing cabinet standing against one wall. "Get hold of the other side," he said, and they manhandled the cabinet away so that the wall-to-wall carpet could be rolled back; but only as far as the desk. They rolled it, and Roger said, "The desk—about a yard." That would be sufficient, the loosened boards lay directly under there.

Now on the desk, together with the normal blotter, in- and out-trays, and various papers, were on the far side a few wilting roses in a vase, put there by the red-haired girl, who did these little things; and on Roger's side a cracked plastic developing tank and the tube of impact glue that he had used to repair it. Let's be truthful: His job left him plenty of idle time, and he fiddled about with bits of photographic equipment in the office as other men practice golf shots.

These things should have been removed before the desk was shifted, but it was a time of high tension. Your seasoned pro can cope with tension. Your amateur wants to be in and out, clutching his guilty secret. He does not want to use time transporting bits and pieces from a desk to the top of a filing cabinet. There was nowhere else to put them.

They lifted the desk as it stood, and, of course, the vase fell over. Which meant water gushing, and an instinctive jerk by the alderman to keep it from soaking his privates. Nervous men jerk heavily. The desk tilted; everything shifted. On Roger's side the developing tank slid. The telephone, the in- and out-trays, everything slid; and the papers were soaked with sudden water. The small tube of glue slid, and fell to the floor unnoticed by either man. Roger, too, was jerking his belly, but forward to use it as a barrier so that the bigger things would not drop. "Watch it, watch it," he hissed—a sure sign of extreme tension, when they hiss without needing to. "Watch it—the papers—the papers—"

"Sod the papers," hissed Alderman Withers. "Move the fucking desk." He never used language like that in the council chamber. And he never hissed.

A yard, and they put the desk down. Roger whipped out his handkerchief to soak up the water, but the alderman, hissing still and wet in the parts his wife had long forgotten, said, "Come on—come on, for Christ's sake."

Roger desisted. The alderman already was rolling his side of the carpet back over the necessary three feet. The fatter man hastened to join in.

In a trice, or little more, they had that carpet rolled and Alderman Withers was bending to keep it in position, because left to itself it will immediately unroll, while Roger lifted out the three loose boards and reached into the cavity between the floor joists and the ceiling to the building-society office beneath; to do which he knelt on the carpet just beyond the roll, reaching over it with one knee on the tube of glue.

He did not, at this time, know it was there. All his mind

was given over to hurrying those packs and boxes out, and getting away from there.

Out from that cavity came four flattish boxes designed for ten-by-eight photographic paper, and three square cardboard boxes, heavier than these. He had to reach well under the secured boards to get them, because here is another strange element in guilt-psychology: he who hides something beneath floorboards will invariably shove it well along, beyond the boards he has loosened. So stretching and grunting were undertaken, with one knee on that tube of glue; which split.

Dimly, he felt sort of a lump, and a wetness at the knee; but there was water about and he was busy, reaching the gear out and handing it to Alderman Withers, who used the calves on his well-turned and silk-socked legs (silk underpants, too, at the top) to hold the carpet steady while he took them; able by twisting the upper part of his body to put them on the desk, until Roger said, "That's the lot," and straightened to full kneeling position, and started to replace the loose boards. Then he began—they both began—to roll the carpet back over. And he said, "What's —I'm stuck."

"Stuck?" said Alderman Withers. Absently, his mind on other things. "Shove the sodding thing," he added, "don't just sit there."

Roger was not, of course, sitting. He was kneeling, but trifling inaccuracies often creep in when people speak under stress. Nor could he push the carpet any further, having come to full stretch and found that he could proceed no longer, being inexplicably fastened by the knee. He made the mistake of feeling, to see what was holding him down.

Now modern impact glue has this in common with old-fashioned marmalade: The second it is broached, you find it all over the place. To some extent this holds true for honey, and some say for strawberry jam; but nothing compares with marmalade save only impact glue, which has a second property, all its own.

Whatever presents a surface to it is snapped at instantly, and held faster, much faster, than it would be in the tentacles of an irate octopus. There is actually a television commercial that shows a sixteen-stone man suspended by his teeth from a strap under a rising helicopter. What unites strap and helicopter? Impact glue, the New Improved Formula.

This tube split at the bottom, as they do when knee-pressed with the cap on, and squirted sideways; so there was Roger now, glued firmly to the carpet not only by knee, but by one hand. He said: "What the—I'm stuck." And, as realization dawned: "The glue—the glue!" And when he had tugged: "Ow! Oo—owow. The bloody glue."

"What glue?" said the alderman.

"On the floor. I'm kneeling in it—and my hand—" He tugged again; and that does hurt, if not done judiciously. "Oo—oh oh—help me—help me—"

Alderman Withers did try to help. As soon as he understood the situation, he came round the desk and tried to prize the fat man free. It was hopeless. If that glue will hold a man suspended by his teeth from a helicopter, it will certainly stick one firmly to the thick, fluffy pile of a carpet. And all this time, the policemen were waiting in the hall downstairs, where Pete Parsons was saying,

"They're a bloody long time. Give him a couple of minutes, and if he hasn't come out, I'll go up."

Four minutes passed, actually, during which the alderman, upstairs, had suggested cutting the carpet away from around Roger—which was patently ridiculous, since they had nothing with which to do it, and anyway it would have left him crouched with a hand beside his knee—and had pulled at him from all angles, without result. They were snarling at each other now, in hisses.

The trouble with Fate, or whatever, is that once it sets this kind of caper into an ongoing posture, it doesn't know when to stop. Or perhaps the matter gets beyond control. Thus Alderman Withers, with one foot on each side of Roger's fat body, desisted at last from trying to free him and hissed:

"Listen—you'll have to stay here—I'll have to get rid of the stuff—I'll come back—bring some stuff to unstick you—" What stuff? There is stuff, people who stick their eyelids and fingers together have it used upon them at hospitals. But is it freely available?

"No," said Roger. "No—you can't leave me here—"

"I won't be long, I won't be long." Fact is, the alderman was sweating richly now with sheer panic. "I'll just—nobody can come in—I'll relock the door—" What he craved was to be gone.

"No—no—" said Roger.

Downstairs, Pete was saying: "Sod this—I'll go up. You two stay here." This was because one man arriving with a smile is a casual caller. Three policemen barging in, one uniformed, is a definite visitation. So the inspector turned to mount the stairs alone.

Alderman Withers was gathering the boxes together and babbling at the babbling Roger that he would be back soon when Pete arrived outside, to find the door locked. Ah now, he thought—why would that be? They must be in there. Shall I go down again, and wait? Or shall I knock, shake 'em up a bit?

I'll knock. Then, if they don't answer, I'll go down. They *must* be up to something funny. Startle 'em a bit, they may do something foolish, come racing out in a muck sweat or something.

He bunched his knuckles and knocked, loudly, at which

Roger and the alderman stiffened in shock. It made no difference to Roger's situation; but Mr. Withers, boxes and packs balanced by now in his arms, had one foot on the edge of the hole. He started so violently that the foot slipped. The boxes flew, prints scattering when the flatter ones hit the ground and lost their lids.

In the office beneath, startled typists jerked round eyes upward as a well-turned and silk-stockinged leg crashed through the ceiling and waved about. Pity it didn't happen earlier, it would have made their entire day. Now, five minutes before release time, the quicker-witted among them rose, making for the door. The slower took their cue, and came behind in a flock.

Pete, when it became apparent that nobody was going to answer his knock, turned and moved to the stairs; halfway down which he came face to face with eight pretty typists, all rushing up. "Hello," he said. "What's on?"

"A leg has fallen through the ceiling," they said. Not in the exact words, eight excited typists all talking at once are not so succinct. But this was the gist of it. Sergeant Wammo Wimbush and PC Dave Hodgekiss heaved in sight now at the bottom of the stairs, come to see what was happening. The inspector addressed them.

"Constable—keep these girls here. Sergeant—come with me."

The policemen pushed through. Constable Hodgekiss stood on the stairs with his arms outstretched, saying: "Now, girls—now, girls." The sergeant traveled on, in the wake of Pete Parsons, who was already manipulating the door lock with the edge of his Barclay Card by the time he arrived. There's nothing to those daft little locks, you know. You can open them with a hairpin, a nail file, almost anything, provided you know how. And policemen pick up all sorts of useful little tricks. It's the company they keep.

Nobody in the outer office. Who thought there would be? They went straight on, to open the inner door. Roger, kneeling by the roll of carpet, goggled at them. Beyond him the trunk of Alderman Withers protruded from the cavity where those boards had been removed; and his contorted face was turned to heaven, the mouth forming strangled bleats of agony because when he fell through the ceiling he landed on his roly-polies astride a beam. Women who prate of the agony of childbirth just don't know, that's all. They just don't know. No wonder his leg waved about. Pete spoke.

"Good evening, gentlemen. Aerobics?"

A few seconds later, when the situation was clarified, he and Sergeant Wammo leaned against Roger's displaced desk and laughed like drains; after which, mopping away tears, he added, "Better see if we can get you out of there, Mr. Withers. Don't know about you, Roj—I think we'll have to ring the hospital, see what they advise." No need now to pussy-foot the alderman. He was not stuck in that hole as part of his service to the community.

It took the solid strength of both policemen to extricate the suffering man, retching and moaning in the sheer hell of his flattened testicles. They should have attended to him immediately, by rights, instead of leaning weakly against that desk convulsed with laughter; but there you are, we all have our faults. Now, Pete crossed to the telephone. A call to the hospital did seem a good idea, in the interests of both these men.

Wammo had moved to pick up the ten-by-eight photographs, scattered on the floor. Looking at them, he said, "Bloody hell!"

It was not the pornographic nature of the pictures that shook him. He expected that, he and Pete both. No, it wasn't that. It was the personnel involved.

# ·18·

The Chief Constable of all the county sat at the Assistant Chief Constable's desk, a man built square and solid, hands richly backed with fur. He was using these hands now to sort through the photographs, the boxes containing videotapes set to one side of the flatter packs. He said,

"We'll have to sit on it all, you understand, until we hear from Whitehall. National security, all that sort of thing."

"Naturally, sir," said the ACC. He was closeted with the great man in his comfortable office, together with the officers involved in the case. He, and they, had sat twice through showings of those astonishing and highly unsavory videos— once in the course of normal duty, and again, when they realized the implications of what they had here, for the benefit of the hastily notified Chief, who drove out from the city HQ immediately. He spoke again now.

"Nothing to the press, nothing to anybody. The PM will want to see them, no doubt. We've got a national scandal here."

They certainly had. Cavorting on the videos, and up to all sorts of tricks with four young ladies—three slim and agile, one over-plump but quite lovely with her clothes off—was Hugo Wendall, and he was the town MP. But bigger yet—his good friend and often weekend guest, a well-known Cabinet Minister, ministering enthusiastically and stalwartly to the plump girl, the slim girls in succession, and even, briefly, to his friend. Oh yes, they were all in together. The girls wore little carnival masks, but nobody doubted who they were. Certainly, a mole on the upper arm of one matched one noted upon the body of Deborah Hollowbone. The Chief said, moving on from one picture to the next:

"Develop early these days, don't they? Fourteen, fifteen, eh? And you say one of them was found dead and the others are her friends?"

"The one with the mole, sir. Deborah Hollowbone. Not much doubt about it. We have the others downstairs." With their parents—lady policemen—all the bods who must be present when juveniles and questioning detectives get together.

"Mm." The Chief's eyes were scanning the new picture. "Mm. Variations, eh? Not particular, are they?"

The new picture showed a quartet. Taken at a different session? More likely than not—surely an aging MP and a still more aging Cabinet Minister could never summon power enough to cope with it all on the same night. If they could, it says a lot for the House of Commons canteen oysters. Bully for them, we should all be so lucky.

This new quartet was all male. No bed featured, the only visible furniture being a cushioned couch and an armchair, on and over both of which the representatives of HM Government were doing things that do not bear thinking about, in conjunction with two naked young men, one slim and slight and pale, the other a veritable young stud. And neither of these was masked. The ACC said,

"We have one of them, sir. Schoolboy, name of Paul Ross. Sergeant Wimbush believes he knows the other. He was with two of the girls and the Ross boy at a disco. The sergeant was investigating the matter of the Hollowbone girl's death. The one with the mole."

"Uh-huh." The furry hands brought another picture to the top of the pack. Yet another variation: mild enough, no doubt, by professional porn standards, but bizarre in a home movie. It was very good of the Cabinet Minister, but of course he could never use it on his election posters. It showed his better profile, eyes glazed and mouth half open as he was manipulated by a masked and mature lady who was herself being ministered to by a fresh participant, the MP grinning naked in the background. "And who is the older woman?"

"We don't know yet, sir," the ACC said. "But we think we can identify the dog."

"Uh-huh. And your murdered man Herbert Fish—you believe he was involved in this?"

"We do, sir." Herbert—Albert—who cares, when the mighty speak? "And our dead girl—pretty certainly the one with the mole."

"Mm. Hmm. Well—I think you are right—a blackmail gang. Whether financial or political remains to be found out."

"We're working on it, sir," the ACC told him. And they were. Downstairs, in addition to the girls and Paul Ross, sat Roger Dunbutt in his spare trousers. It took some time and considerable effort to release him from the carpet and apply bandages to skinned knee and hand. The ambulance that brought a young lady doctor to deal with it then took Alderman Withers and a constable to the hospital, for attention to his mashed parts. He would be back shortly. As soon as this Chief Constable's conference was over, hard questioning would be resumed.

"And you think both deaths are connected?"

"We think so, sir. We believe both victims fell foul somehow of the blackmail gang."

"Well—mm. Nothing to the press, then. Nothing to anybody. We're mucking about with dynamite. Good show.

Good show. But er—mm. Suggest we all go downstairs, start gathering up the details. And—er—better have a car, get this lot up to London. Have the stills copied, for our files." Never let devastating material pass into the hands of politicians without proof that it exists—or existed—firmly locked away. And be sure delivery is signed for. Legibly.

Everything had been suspended, awaiting the Chief Constable's arrival and reaction. Now the team moved swiftly again, making up for lost time. The Chief himself went down to the cells with his assistant, and both loomed terrifyingly in the background while Superintendent Ted Churchyard, knees and elbows and all, leaned very hard upon the sweating, bleating Roger. People like Roger cannot stand up to people like the police, especially when the latter appear in majesty. The limp and juddering fat man began to sing through his tears even before Alderman Withers was brought back from hospital, and long before Pete Parsons and Wammo returned.

These two shot straight off, armed with two hurriedly procured search warrants. First to Roger's house, where they were followed about by his crook-backed and chumbling old mum, on the ground floor only. She couldn't get up the stairs to where her idolized offspring's darkroom was. Her dim, arthritis-ridden decrepitude, her idolization, without doubt were the factors that allowed him to pursue his interests untrammeled. They left with very little. A few relatively innocent prints and negs of naked boys and girls, some below even the age of puberty. All the juicy stuff, obviously, Roger kept under the office floor. And that young red-haired girl walking about above it all this time, in her sweet innocence. It doesn't bear thinking about.

From here, they went to Alderman Withers' beautiful house, set discreetly in its own extensive grounds. They were admitted—couldn't keep them out, could she? Not when they flashed the warrant—by Mrs. Withers. She shut the dog in the kitchen. It seemed a very friendly creature, standing tall when it began, with no introduction, to frot against the sergeant's leg.

A tough-fibered lady, this. Went grim when told of her husband's accident and arrest. Knew nothing. Absolutely nothing. He lived his life, she lived hers. Certainly they had entertained the MP. Often, and the Cabinet Minister several times. To dinner, her husband was after all a local politician of substance. They might do well to remember that. After dinner? Ridiculous. Yes, she often left them talking when she went to bed. Politics.

They went all over that beautiful house. The alderman, too, had a darkroom, but with nothing hair-raising in it. The lady stood by while they checked, Wammo Wimbush noted, in other parts of the house, things that interested him; but he kept his mouth shut. It was, after all, Pete's caper. No doubt, he, too, had noted. Let him run it his way.

Mind you, it was not *his* way. He would have shot over here with a heavy squad, he'd have torn the place apart. But again, he found in Pete this disinclination to lean. Indeed, after what seemed to him a very cursory skim of the premises, the inspector apologized tamely for bothering the lady, and left her to do what she liked with whatever was hanging about. The sergeant could not resist a note of implied reproof as they drove away. He said,

"That was the couch, you know, in that little room next to the attic. And the armchair. Downstairs, in the guest room."

"Uh-huh," said Pete. "And they took the stuff in that attic room. One-way, that big mirror on the wall; picture in the next room backs right onto it. That's where they shot from. They'd have moved the furniture in and out as they wanted it, returned the attic junk afterwards."

"Why didn't we move the picture, then?" Reasonable. A big one-way mirror between adjoining attic rooms is pretty damning.

"Because she's a stubborn old cow. Because she can clam up and deny all knowledge. If she clams, even if somebody else tries to shop her, we'll have a sod of a job to keep her on the hook. Money there—it'll buy some very fancy lawyers."

Fair enough again. Sufficient money, you can get away with murder. People have done it. But Wammo said, "If we'd run her in on suss, we could have done her over before we allowed her a brief."

"True. True."

Wammo waited a moment, expecting more. It didn't come. He said, "What's the betting she's starting a bloody great bonfire right now?" Of stuff kept, perhaps, in a safe— little notebooks, maybe masses of useful porn. Sod it, they hadn't even looked for a safe, or asked if there was one.

"Forensic'll work wonders with the ashes. We've more than enough to nail her husband; and how splendid if we can show that she went to work to destroy incriminating matter, soon as we left."

"She'll sling the bloody ashes in the dustbin."

"So they'll work wonders with the dustbin. Stop here. Make a U-turn." They were nicely along the street. A U-turn brought the house driveway comfortably under observation. No craning, they could loll there looking through the windscreen. "Good. Get on the squeaker. Three men in a car, they can park it round the corner. One for the back of the house, one in the front garden, one to stay with the car. We'll hang on here until they arrive."

He could have made the call himself, the mike hung equidistant between the car seats. But there you are, he didn't. When the sergeant put the mike down, he—the sergeant— said,

"I don't get it. We could take her in on suss. Wouldn't mind betting it's her in the bloody photo."

"What do you suggest, then, that we ask her to strip and kneel down while we view her from the rear? Wouldn't do much good if we did, you can't see all that much of her because of the dog."

"Bloody dog!" said Wammo. Exclaimed it. "Dirty bastard!"

"Didn't you enjoy it? I thought you did."

"Turn it up. Not even a bitch." And now Wammo grinned, widely. "Nothing queer about Carruthers."

Two policemen, sitting in a parked car and laughing. It happens more often than you may think. And the joke is usually off-color. It moves the mind away, that's the thing. Moves it for as long as the joke can be made to last away from the job's intrinsic nastiness.



It is rarely a pretty sight when a soft villain splits. Your true pro accepts as part of the game that he can be lumbered, and when he is, he carries it well; but Roger was amateur, and fat with it. He sang in a welter of tears and rank sweat, prodded onward by Ted Churchyard while the grim top brass leaned silent against the wall of the interview room and a copper sat hunched on a small wooden chair, taking it all down in shorthand. This was the burden of his song:

Long ago, when he joined the Camera Club, he and fellow-member Alderman Withers, chumming up as men already known to each other through the working overlap of profession and charity interest, revealed to each other by degrees a shared interest in mild pornography. The usual thing: young people. Prepubertals. Each had a small collection. Soon, they were having little sessions together, Alderman Withers gathering the naughty little models from somewhere, Roger said he didn't know where. Sometimes they used the alderman's house, when Mrs. Withers had gone away, or to bed. Smuggled the kids in blindfold. Sometimes they used Roger's house, his mum in bed or downstairs too besotted to ask questions, quite unable to come up. No problems, everything very private, all the necessary taking and processing equipment in their respective houses.

Then Albert copped in. One of Roger's regulars, just come from a spell of porridge. Called while Roger was out—and dammit, that red-haired girl showed him into the inner office and left him to wait, closing the door behind her. Quick as a flash—it must have been—Albert was through the desk drawers, in one of which, well hidden, was a packet containing fruit of last night's session, which Roger intended to dribble over with Mr. Withers by appointment later in the day. They could always fix privacy, at the town hall. Confidential chat regarding some old lag. Everybody knew Roger, everybody knew of the alderman's charitable works. He certainly did not hide them. See that I'm not disturbed, Miss Williams; I'll be in with Mr. Dunbutt.

Now these snaps, unfortunately, were not yet trimmed, and on one, other side of the three gamboling children, was unmistakably Alderman Withers, operating his own camera. It often happened that in moving around for various shots, one or both caught the other on the fringes. They trimmed such appearances off in each other's presence, from print and negative both. At this stage, the prints were untouched.

Albert probably had no time to pocket them and use them to put a direct bite on. He was sifting through them when Roger came back and grabbed them. But, of course, the game was blown.

But Albert, too, bent as a brush in every direction, had salacious interest in pornography; and because he knew the profit in it and had bent contacts everywhere, instead of the bite as Roger and later Alderman Withers feared, he made certain suggestions.

So now they were in business, in a small but surprisingly lucrative way. And then Albert went to jail again, for an unrelated matter concerned with his normal thief's trade; and the porno game languished until he came out. When they got him the job as caretaker at the Queen Victoria School.

Not with intent, Roger swore; it just happened that the job was vacant. It was Albert, he said, who recruited the girls, entirely off his own bat. No, he—Roger—didn't know how he did it. He just did, and at first he, Roger, and Withers did not even realize they were town girls.

And yes—Albert got married. His wife might have helped, even advised him; she worked as a cook up there. Now she did part time at the birth-control clinic. He thought she must have known all about it, because when he expressed fear that the girls might become pregnant, Albert said it was all taken care of.

The politicians were insinuated into sessions by Alderman Withers. Yes—oh yes—(the fat man was weeping hard now)—blackmail. No—they hadn't done anything with them yet—Alderman Withers' idea, it was all Alderman Withers' idea—they took them through his one-way mirror. . . .

That was Roger's story, so far as it went, before he collapsed completely. By the time he was done with, Pete Parsons and Wammo Wimbush were on the way back from the With-

'ers' house, in time to sit in upon the questioning of the alderman himself, returned from hospital with a limp and none of his usual politician's bonhomie.


They'd had to put the alderman in a cell, all the interview rooms being occupied. By the time all the policemen were in, it was quite crowded. The poor man kept bleating that he wanted his solicitor present, but the weight of a Chief Constable can squash that, especially when he is able to quote the Official Secrets Act. Policemen like to keep the lawyers at bay as long as possible. They do so complicate matters.

The alderman, once they had stripped him of the erroneous belief that he possessed these statutory rights, jellified almost as rapidly as Roger had when the shorthand policeman read that man's statement to him. Most of his own song echoed Roger's; but he added little trills and fattened a bar or two. Like—

He said yes—he'd known the town MP since they were on the council together. They'd business interests in common and—certain types of photographs—yes. No—the MP didn't know, when he, the alderman, invited him to enjoy certain— activities—that he was being photographed. And he brought his other friend, the Minister.

No—not blackmail. Not for money. He'd just thought they might be—useful. Politically. He meant to stand for Parliament, next election. The pictures might have persuaded Mr. Wendall to stand down. And the Minister to—well, both of them—to—use influence. Back him. Not that he really meant to use them, it was a—joke.

Really, the things people say when they sit sweating and quivering about the jowls on the board bunk of a naked cell, with coppers all around. Just about here, yet another appeared, very apologetically—it's a thick man condemned to lowly rank who barges in upon godlike brass without apology—to say that a call was coming in for Chief Inspector Parsons, who tiptoed away forthwith.

He returned just as the alderman, on a quaking vibrato, returned to his sub-theme with a grace-note added. He wanted his lawyer. And his wife—he wanted to ring his wife. Beautifully cued in, the inspector made his little warble.

"You'd find nobody there, sir. Your wife ordered a taxi. My men just pulled her out of it. She had hand luggage and over thirty thousand pounds in her handbag. The driver says he was to take her to the city airport."

Thirty thousand quid, thought Wammo, in the small silence while the alderman's eyes goggled. Stone me! I *said* we ought to have looked for a safe. Mind you, he's a crafty old bugger, is Pete. Can't say now she didn't know it was there, can she? Can't play the innocent. The innocent don't try to scarper.

Ted Churchyard, another man quick to pick up a cue, spoke quietly, as though he'd expected it. "Now why do you suppose she would be doing that?"

Mr. Withers knew, all right. Here was the betrayal that finally destroyed him. He burst out: "The cow! The cow! It was her—it was her—she did it—she did all the business—"

"If you are wise, Mr. Withers," the lanky man said, "you will make a full statement before she has a chance to make one laying it all on you."

They are very professional, the police. Every man there would have moved on it just as smoothly to exploit this sudden windfall. Every man there had done it often, every man there still working in the field—chief constables and ACCs have gone beyond it—would do it often again. Divide and conquer.

* * *

Nobody doubted, as the alderman made his statement, that this was the truth so far as he knew it. His wife, he said, was in from the very beginning—she it was who encouraged his porno interests in the early days of marriage, she was his first model, she and her bloody dog. Not this one, but this one was as bad. And when Albert went to jail last time, she took over the marketing. Keen business woman—his legitimate success owed much to her—she expanded it all.

No, he didn't know how, she didn't tell him everything. London—she made contacts in London. She took the material up—he didn't know where—and they copied it there, he supposed. They'd have sold it overseas—he didn't know—but they paid. Big sums. Albert and Roger got 50 percent between them.

No—they didn't sell the ones featuring Mr. Wendall and the Minister. She shared his political ambitions; these were quite separate. She suggested it for—because they might be useful.

Here, Pete Parsons asked a question. "Did she take part in these sessions?"

Answer: "One. Only one. She said that one a little—warmer—could do no harm."

"This is the picture with the dog?"

"Yes. Yes."

"Did Mr. Dunbutt take this one?"

"No. He wasn't there. I took it."

Superintendent Churchyard: "Carry on, Mr. Withers. She made contacts in London. You don't know who with?"

"No. But I think Tony Conti does."

"Who is Tony Conti?"

"He came—she brought him back—he appeared after

she went to London. I think they sent him to—represent them. Look after their—interests. He was in—some of the—"

The stud, Wammo thought. The beefcake in the gay quartet—the lad I saw with the girls, at the Blue Grotto. And chummy here didn't mean to say that, which is why he broke off; because if the stud performed with the politicos, and the stud is organization man—organization knows about the politicos. Doesn't it?

Ted Churchyard speaking again. "You say you don't know anything about your London contacts. Names—addresses—anything like that?"

"No. She does—she knows the addresses. She must do—she took the stuff."

"And what," said the superintendent, "about the dead girl? And Albert Fish?"

"Ah—hah—" the alderman said, popped with quick sweat and goggling anew. The abrupt switch in emphasis seemed to catch him off balance, to prod the rage out of him. Suddenly guarded again, he said, "I don't know anything about that."

"I hope you'll be able to prove it in court." Even in the presence of Ultimate Brass, high rank may clip the book a little. How else could you get results? "I expect we will be charging you with Mr. Fish's murder."

"M-murder? No—why would I—"

"We believe he was blackmailing you. We believe he was putting the bite on. That's why he visited you and Mr. Dunbutt. Isn't it?"

"No—I—not—he was frightened—he was afraid you would be investigating up at the school—frightened of— She did it—she said he was dangerous. She said she'd get Tony Conti to—warn him off. And then we—I—heard Albert was— I didn't have anything to do with it, I swear it. On my life—"

"And where does this Tony Conti live?" asked Superintendent Churchyard.

# ·19·

Chief Inspector Parsons managed a brief call to his wife before he left the station. He said, "Sorry, love—looks as if I'm going to be late again."

"What is it this time?" she asked. Never a girl to pout, nevertheless there are times when the best of police wives comes close to it.

"Can't tell you that," he said. "All under wraps. Just got to go and collect a character; I'll be home as soon as I can."

"Blame yourself if dinner's spoiled. You can't reheat shepherd's pie, you know."

That's all there was to that. As he put the phone down, he said to Wammo Wimbush, "Want to give Dot a bell, tell her you'll be late?"

"She'll know, won't she?" said Wammo. "Soon as I don't come home."

Somebody had to go and gather this Tony Conti. Wammo was obvious choice for one, because he knew how the lad looked with his clothes on. And Pete—well, top rank on a murder case will make his arrests in person when he can. With the very top man tied up, as Ted Churchyard was, and the second-in-command superfluous to HQ probing, a nod sends the man forth, and happy to be at work rather than leaning on a wall listening to the work being done, cheek by jowl with God and Assistant God.

They took with them one driver, chauffeuring the official car; and a second car holding two more uniform men. Villains like to see a uniform or two when they are arrested, it seems to settle them. Faced witih plainclothes only, they tend more to violence, and that's how they get their noses broken. This arrestee would have uniforms enough. His friendly neighborhood beat car had been diverted and was already parked unobtrusively at the end of his street.

They are tall, thin houses along Sibbal Street, built at the turn of the century and carved now into flats. Rather nice flats, private and well suited to such as can afford to pay for service, which includes a beady lady lurking in the basement area, peering and cleaning and reporting to the owners in the manner of the French concierge.

The lady in this house popped out when the police came through the front door and into the hall, two big plainclothes, one fair-sized uniform man. One uniform man was gone to the back garden, via an alleyway. One stood out front. The beat car remained in its out-of-sight parking spot. The woolly-cardiganed, slippered, and gin-scented lady said, "What do you want?"

"Police," said Inspector Parsons.

"Well, I can see that," she said. "I'm not bloody daft."

"Is Mr. Conti in?" They knew this was the house, his name was on a pasteboard card beside one of the bell-pushes.

"I suppose so," she said. "Why, what's he done?"

They did not say murdered Albert, we believe, among other things. Pete said, "Stay down here, madam, please," and they left her there, standing in her slippers in the hall. Which she kept very nicely, in spite of her faults, many of which were gin-based.

Second floor, the pasteboard name-card said. They mounted the stairs, carpet muffling their footsteps. Three smartly painted doors leading off from the landing, each bearing a small name-tag. "This is it," Pete whispered. "Stay close to the wall." He knocked, a soft *rat-tat-tat*. And he'd picked a bad time.

The man Conti was sitting in his living room quietly and peaceably reloading his gun. At least once a day he did maintenance on his gun, with love. He had stripped it, cleaned it, reassembled it, and was poking the last bullet into the clip when the knock came. He stiffened. Rarely did anybody knock on his door. Silence; and a repeat knock.

He rose to his feet, stood looking a moment toward the front door. Then he stuffed the gun under a settee cushion and went to answer.

Perhaps he should not have done that, perhaps he should have stayed quiet, in the hope that whoever it was would go away. They wouldn't have gone off, of course; but he'd have given himself time to think, they might have drawn back believing they'd have to watch and wait for him to come home. Mind you, he did not entirely believe it was the police. The criminal mind automatically jumps to them when a knock comes unexpectedly; but this was not a peremptory knock, and there'd been no hint that they were thinking about him.

When the door opened, an inch or two only, the man outside said mildly, "Good evening. Mr. Conti?"

"Yeah. Yeah. Who's asking?" The accent, the phrasing, were American. This might have warned Pete Parsons; even in this day of universal violence, the American criminal is rather freer with the gun than is the British.

"We are the police—"

Maybe the man panicked. After all, he was the one who knew what had happened to Albert. And to others. And his record and present whereabouts were matters of interest, not as yet to British police, but to Interpol and the FBI.

Or maybe he did not panic. He was a man bred and trained to violence, a longtime devotee of the gun; and the mind attuned by nature to violence thinks in violent terms. The gun had extricated him from awkward situations before.

He tried to slam the door. Even in this he was violent. A simple push might have done it; but he drew it back to slam it, and a policeman's foot slides in rapidly, given a gap. His shoulder moves, also, to bounce the door back.

And now he turned, to scramble back into the living room and to scramble under that cushion, the fool, while Pete teetered for a moment off-balance before he could follow, Wammo close behind, and the uniform man bringing up the rear.

"Now don't be foolish, lad," said the inspector, when he found himself looking into the black, ugly thing. It checked him, just inside the living room door. And he was in order, when he said "lad," the lad was surely no older than twenty-two, twenty-three. Five at the outside.

"Another step—another step—" the husky young man said, meaning, quite obviously: Don't take one.

Pete took one; but not coming straight. Head down, crouched like a rugby footballer, he swerved; and this was hard luck for Wammo, looming in the doorway. The gun cracked, and he said quite softly, "Oh Christ," just as the inspector's shoulder hit the young man and his fist followed, such a right hook as is rarely seen in televised boxing.

Completely concentrated, Pete did not hear him, nor the slithering sound as he slid down the doorjamb. He was hooking the lad again. It is doubtful if the lad heard anything, either. He was unconscious already when the gun flew from his hand and he staggered back, to crash through the window.

Pete leapt; grabbed him by his left ankle, just in time to save him from smashing head-first onto concrete two floors below. The uniform policeman also leapt—it was so quick, so confused (less shock, and he might have stopped to minister to Wammo)—across the room to the window, out of which he leaned, never mind the jagged shards, to grab the right ankle. Pete could never have held the weight on his own, the first attempt had jerked him halfway through the shattered frame.

The thing about Wammo: He made no fuss. Clearly, he did not realize how seriously he was shot, or didn't want to interfere with the arrest, or he was in shock. He sat on the floor blinking down at the blood pumping from his thigh to soak his trousers; while his two fellow policemen struggled to haul that heavy, supine body back through a destroyed and shard-stuck window. It is highly probable that he would have sat and quietly died there, had it not been for that lady left in the hall.

Ladies with gin-blur on them, commanded to stay downstairs in their own houses, tend not to stay there. This one mounted, and was on the landing when the big men rushed into the American's flat. She heard the shot, followed immediately by the smashing of glass. This is what brought her in: They were smashing up her flat. Well, not hers, exactly; but she was responsible. The idea that she might get shot never occurred to her, she was bridled with gin-indignation.

The shriek she gave when she came upon the man sitting on the floor was not entirely due to the ruinous blood spreading all over a nice buff carpet; it was more because— count it to her credit—before he died from a fishbone stuck in the throat she'd had a husband, enthusiast in the St. John's Ambulance Brigade, who had bashed her bored ear for years with gruesome relish and had used her for practice, paying particular attention to wounds and the bandaging of upper thighs and bosoms and the like in the heady days of a short engagement, and even in the early days of marriage before he took to misogamy and she to gin. Something from those days stuck; she knew a severed vein when she saw it. Rushing into the bedroom, she shrieked: "A femoral, a femoral! Get his trousers off! Get his trousers off!" And she began to tear up a sheet.

Pete and the constable had manhandled the sagging body in through the window by now. Supporting it between them, they glanced round. "Christ!" Pete said, when he saw all the blood; while the uniform man let go and sprang across the room to where Wammo looked up at him and said, "I'm all right, mate—I'm all right." He then rolled his eyes upward and sagged sideways.

Policemen know what to do, in cases like this. They are trained to the basic first-aid skills and matured in them by road accidents. By the time the lady came with her strips of sheet, the constable had his sergeant's trousers down and his thumbs were pressing, his truncheon out and ready to aid with the tourniquet. The husky young villain, well clobbered, lolled against the wall under the window, abandoned when Pete leapt to the telephone, to dial 999 and to shout: "Ambulance—and don't hang about. Twenty-eight Siddal Street—femoral—bring a doctor—tell him it's a severed femoral." Instinctive chauvinism. There are plenty of good female doctors around.

# ·20·

It was later even than Pete had prophesied when he came home, and tonight Suzie could offer no comfort. Breasts, womb, and warm kissing were normally efficacious when he came in tightened by things seen and experienced; but she had sense enough not to shove them at him now. This was a time of shock, a time to listen—to prompt—to let him talk himself over it, if he could. Afterwards—if the afterwards seemed right for it—she would lay her body down with his, and love him back to balance, and use her arms to hold him through the night.

The need to do it was more than usually urgent in her, because tonight brought bludgeoning into her mind the fear always there, resolutely wrestled into a back compartment. It might so easily have been him who was shot—and killed— bleeding to death—bloody ruin where his beautiful face used to be, all the white teeth smashed and broken—all the lovely, flat-muscled soft-haired belly ripped away by the shotgun blast. Every loving police wife fights her leering imagination these days whenever she waves her man off to work. Perhaps this is why so much of the talk between them is joky. Poor jokes, for the most part; except that no jest made in love is a poor one. Not in the true sense. The cumulative effect of many loving jokes between loving people is a piling up of riches.

But there were no jokes tonight. He hardly touched his

supper—it wasn't shepherd's pie, that was just one of her jokes, put in to shove away the creep of fear when she knew something had blown up and he was off on an arrest—and now the television fluttered ridiculous in the living room, miming with the sound turned down.

He was pacing—pacing—while she sat in her armchair watching him, noting the strain in his face. He was saying, not for the first time:

"We should have had guns. I did it—I did for poor old Wammo—if we'd had guns, it wouldn't have happened; we'd have had the bastard down."

"You couldn't know," she said; and this, too, not for the first time. "How were you to know he was dangerous?"

"Of course I should have known. It's big, it's the biggest thing ever. Special Branch is on it—the Vice Squad in London—they're talking about the bloody Mafia, this Conti geezer's supposed to be Mafia. It's gone all the way to Interpol—the bloody FBI." Then, remembering again that he should not be telling her this, with the bar gone up: "Don't say anything to *anybody* about *anything*. You'll get me done."

Under the Official Secrets Act, what's more. Finis to any career. He knew what he knew only because he rang Ted Churchyard from the hospital, where he went with Sergeant Wimbush—and stayed. Wouldn't leave—minutes only before the bar went up. The fact that it was up reached the superintendent's ear while he was actually speaking. He broke the talk off, warned Pete; but by then he had revealed things, as he was bound normally to do to his co-worker.

He said that Mrs. Withers, told of the shooting and the arrest of the man Conti, had started on her own song at last. And *she* said the photographs and video material featuring the politicians went up to London without her husband's knowing—she took it, and brought it back when the people in

London were done with it. Presumably they copied it, and had copies now. She didn't know—they, through Conti, suggested embroiling the politicians in the first place. All she knew was: They paid well, and she salted it away separately.

She gave the London address; and Scotland Yard, already alerted, flipped through its Special Branch files and found that they had the building listed as belonging to the Mafia.

So it was all very hot; and Suzie said now, "Of course I won't tell anybody. What do you think I am?" A moment, while he paced; and she added, "What will they do with the stuff, then?"

"How the hell do I know?" he snapped. "All John le Carré country, that is. But it's got to be useful, hasn't it, holding the bite on top politicians? Maybe they'll flog it to whoever can use it—Russia. The bloody opposition, for all I know. Send 'em to newspapers, when they want to hit the government. I don't know how they operate, I'm just a thick-headed copper. It's all down to Special Branch, now. They're flogging straight porn all over the world, aren't they?" He pawed at an itchy ear with one of his bandaged hands; looked at his jacket, cut all down the front and slung onto a chair. "Made a bloody mess of my jacket," he said.

Be glad you were wearing it, she thought. I am—you could have ripped your stomach open. Or— "You were lucky," she said. "You could have slashed your wrists." People die, they commit suicide like that.

"Yeah. I know." Now he grinned, for the first time since he came in. "That'd have been a situation, wouldn't it, Wammo and me both at it when the gear arrived. They were only catering for one. Wonder who they'd have let go, him or me?"

"Not very funny," she said.

"Wasn't really meant to be. I suppose somebody would

have had it." He paced a little more. "Poor old Albert, he fell in right over his ears." His mind was jumping about, feverishly hopping from facet to facet of the case. "Ted says the Withers woman says they didn't know, him and his old lady. He—and her—they started the game off, but they never knew it had grown. All they got was their little cut."

Ted said that Mrs. Withers said that when Albert paid his visits to Dunbutt and her husband, he was panicking about heavy police questioning close to the source of the porno racket. He went to where he might—by pointing out that if he went down, they all went down—find backing weighty enough to deflect the police from pressing too hard beyond the robbery.

Well, Withers told his wife. Poor man, he told her everything. And she told Conti, who was to scare Albert, rough him up a bit if necessary.

The next thing she knew, she said, Albert was dead. She rang Conti. He told her that he went to call on Albert. A good pro, he spotted the lurking police car, entered by the back door, knocked, and put a gun on Albert, he said to scare him only. Albert, in his panic, fled and fell out of the window before a blow was struck. Conti went to check, down among the dustbins. The man was dead. Conti scarpered. End of story, so far as the lady was concerned. She hadn't been in touch with Conti since.

All this matter Pete had already passed on to Suzie. No need for him to reiterate, no need for him to mention Albert again; but a man on edge talking to his woman will keep talking, over and over the things he has already covered. And she will listen if she loves him, she will even show interest. Suzie said now,

"Well—it looks as if you've got that one cleared."

"I don't know if it does," he said. "It ties in with the

other lark. We may be ordered to drop it, leave it on the files. It's all a bloody mess. What are we going to do about Albert's missus? Charge her with forgery? Let her go? I don't know. And what about the rest of 'em? Do we do 'em for the porn caper, offenses against children? That's going to go big with the media. How will the lads in London sit on the other lark, if that blows up? Kill it, I suppose, under the Official Secrets Act. If this *was* John le Carré, the whole bloody lot of 'em would probably disappear. Save a lot of sweat, wouldn't it? Come to think of it, they may be lucky we picked 'em up, the Mafia might have 'em on the hit list, if they *are* in and they've got what they wanted."

"Seems funny," Suzie said, "your Albert just falling out of the window like that."

"What?" His mind had left Albert. He brought it back. "He didn't; he was coshed. Probably with the gun barrel. This Conti wouldn't have just stepped in. As soon as Albert opened the door, he'd have used his shoulder, if he was there to impress. Gun in Albert's gut, run him back fast across the room, snarl at him, and all that. He probably didn't have time himself to notice the window was open. Albert turns in panic—bomp! Gun across back of head—Albert out of the window. Cock-up. Ted's got Conti, he'll have all the details out of him, believe me. Sod Judge's Rules, the top brass will be slipping out for cocoa about now, let him get on with it in private. If Special Branch hasn't claimed him, them and their rubber hoses."

What Suzie was doing, really, was trying to draw the poison out, all the poison of the day. She fed him another line. "Well, at least Wammo's all right."

"If you can call lying in hospital with a bloody great hole in your leg all right."

"Well, he's going to *be* all right." She did now find a point neither had touched upon. "How's Dot taken it?"

"Came in howling her eyes out."

"Maybe out of evil cometh good. Maybe they'll have a reunion."

They hadn't actually parted, but he knew what she meant. "A few inches higher," he said, "he'd have had nothing to reune with."

Here, the phone rang. He said: "I'll get it," and she watched while he went into the hall, fumbling at the instrument awkwardly with his bandaged hands. When he came back into the living room he said, "Sorry, love, I'll have to go out again."

Now she made her one joke of the evening. Not a big one, nothing to write to *Reader's Digest* about. But then, the old familiar fear was crawling again. "Don't tell me," she said. "Our Gracious Queen's been kidnapped."

# ·21·

The man met him at the door, strain etched deep in his face. Born not many years before Pete, but he looked much older tonight. Sudden shock does that. He said, "Ah—Mr. Parsons. Come in—she wanted you, she said we should ask for you. She's—er—in here." He led the way across a neat little hall, opened a door, and stood aside to let the inspector through.

This room, in more rotund and comfortable days, would have been the Best Parlor. Now, without doubt, they called it the lounge; neatly furnished with an abundance of hire-purchase Leatherette and leatherine, Canaletto prints clinging to the lumpety-bumpety wallpaper. The girl sat in one of the armchairs, her shock-ravaged mother standing behind her with hands on the chair back, as though to protect her vulnerable young against the intruder. Inspector Parsons spoke first to her. "Good evening, madam." And then, to the girl: "Good evening, Patricia. I believe you wanted to see me."

The plump, bespectacled child sat red-eyed and puffy from recent tears, looking at him dumbly. The mother said quietly, "Sit down, Mr. Parsons, won't you? She has something to tell you." Her mouth was tight and trembling.

The inspector sat, in the second leather-type armchair. He said, "I understand you can help us. In the matter of Deborah Hollowbone."

Still the girl held her silence. The father spoke abruptly; sternly, even. "Tell him, Patricia. Tell him what you told us."

"Don't bully her, Daddy," said the woman. "Let her— let her—"

Over her speaking, the girl burst out: "I didn't—she wasn't—it was her fault—and him—it was his fault—" She ended in a storm of sobbing, sitting bolt upright with the tears streaming down her face.

The father stood in tense silence. Her mother hastened to bend over her, drawing the distorted face to her bosom, stroking her hair, murmuring comfort. Pete sat with his bandaged hands in his lap, mentally self-isolated, as a policeman must be or go mad from the pain all around. When the girl was quietened, he said gently, "All right, Patricia. Let's start at the beginning, shall we?"

She told it in jerks, punctuated with tears and bursts of sudden sobbing. It took time. A long, hard day for Pete Parsons. A long, hard day for them all.

She said that Debbie was the recruiting agent, that she was sex-mad and at it long before Albert came and, when he caught her with two boys in the boiler house, where she did it often and bragged of it (Albert didn't catch her, Pete thought; he'd have sneaked and pried, probably armed with information from his new wife, and set her up), he suggested that she oblige friends of his, for money. And then—so Patricia said— that she enlist her friends, Helen and Angie. And herself. Paul Ross was doing it already.

This had been said before, by this child and the others, at the station. The police knew it all: the wages paid, everything. Pete did not, as yet; but he knew he had only to appear at the station or ring in to collect all the details. For now, he was not here working on the sex case. That was all under control, and all the youngsters scot-free; because technically, no offense had been committed *by* them, only against them. Under the age of consent, you cannot nail them even for prostitution. Somebody else would have to prove that they had done it since they turned sixteen. He was here purely to listen. And to prompt, as necessary. Still very gentle, he said now,

"What I want to hear about, Patricia, is the evening Debbie died. Just tell me about that."

Her mother spoke, abruptly and on a hard note. "It was that Paul Ross. He was never any good, I told her so. But she was in love with him. You know what they are—she was in love with him."

Patricia was weeping again. Her father answered for her. "She says she went with Debbie after school. To the woods. They were quarreling."

Pete kept his eyes on Patricia. "What about?"

This time she answered, in an agonized wail. "She—stole him. He was mine—she was doing it with him—I found out—she was doing it with him—they used to do it in the hut in the woods—she was going to meet him there—"

"Taking you with her?" Gloating? The pretty girl triumphing over the plain? The vicious nympho, stealing her fat friend's boy and mockingly offering an exhibition, suggesting friend bend with eye to knothole? Who could tell, they were up to some very nasty capers.

"No—no—I *went* with her, I got on the bus and went with her. She—I wasn't going to let her—she was meeting him—she was laughing—at me—she said did I want to watch—she was—wicked."

"Easy, now—easy. What happened?"

"I—grabbed her tie—I meant to—she was choking—she let go of me to get it loose. I—she fell over the—she fell in—"

The father spoke. "Tell him. Tell him what you told us."

"She—she—" the mother said. He cut in on her, harshly because big boys don't cry.

"She has to tell the truth, Mummy. She mustn't lie anymore."

"I pushed her," Patricia said.

Silence for a moment. Pete said, "What did you do then?"

"I—ran away. I was—scared."

"You didn't go down to see if she was alive?"

"I looked down. She was lying—still. So I—ran away."

Left her there. Wanted her dead. Well—it's all happened before; it will all happen again.

And he was tired. Exhausted by the long, hard day, by the sheer physical and mental labor of it, by the surge of adrenaline and its ebb, by the emotional stress of believing his oppo must die, by the jolting joy of knowing he would not. This stupid, sordid little confession by a stupid, neurotically bent little tart came as anticlimax, serving only to thicken his sudden revulsion against all his work, its eternal involvement with violence and death and all the foulness that festers in the sewer department of human existence. Late at night, sitting bandaged in a Leatherette armchair, he wanted out. He wanted out; and cleanly Suzie, her breasts, her clean womb, her arms, and her sanity. He spoke to the child.

"And it was you who rang me. Twice." In a voice pitched squeaky, like a strangling infant.

"Yes," she said.

"Saying Paul Ross went into the woods with her." Paul Ross. Who may well have seen the girl dead, and also scarpered. The hut was nearby; if he waited and she didn't turn up he may have gone looking for her. Ah well—who cared? Let some other bugger sort it out. "Why did you do that?"

"I thought—because—" She petered into silence.

Because hell hath no fury like a fat girl scorned. Because the bastard must pay. Because in your stupid, obscene little obsession you thought you could turn us away, you thought you could get yourself off the hook and spike him. Ah well—push it to the end.

Very gently, he said, "Why, Patricia? Why did you do that?"

"Why did you?" the mother said. "You didn't tell us about—why? You loved him—"

Girls commonly, in times of stress, turn round on their mothers. This one did, now. "I hated him!" she yelled, suddenly, shockingly. "I hated him! *And* her—the bitch, the dirty, whoring bitch." And then she was sobbing, her head buried in her hands; sobbing: "I love him. He was mine. I love him—"

Hell hath no fury. And in the strange canon of woman, another cliché holds true: For the maternal instinct, there is no cutout point. The woman was on her knees, cradling the child's head again and murmuring to her, while the father stood by, destroyed and helpless amid the shock and wreckage, and the policeman sat in his withdrawn condition of exhaustion; until the girl was quiet again.

Now he stirred. A long day. And not over yet. The girl must be taken in—charged—statements taken, typed, signed. Reports to be made, work to be done stretching far into the night. He must ring Suzie. He addressed the man. "May I use your telephone?"

"Telephone?" the man said. "Ah—yes. It's in the hall. I'll show you."

Pete got up. At the door he turned. One last point to be clarified, because young Ross did not appear only in the pictures featuring the politicians. He was in some of the nonpolitical videos, cavorting with the girls; one certainly Patricia;

one, by the mole on her arm, the dead Debbie, with whom he was shown hard at work. He spoke to Patricia.

"Paul Ross. Why did you object so strongly? You knew he was indulging with her."

Not only with her—with the whole shabby lot of you.

"You don't understand, do you?" she cried. "You don't understand—any of you. That was for *money*. So we could get married. That was only for *money*."